The Masterpiece Beneath

Lisa Buffaloe

The Masterpiece Beneath
John 15:11 Publications
Copyright 2022 Lisa Brewer Buffaloe
All rights reserved.

This novel is a work of fiction. Names, characters, places, countries, and all incidents are the product of the author's imagination and are used fictitiously. Any resemblance to actual events, persons living or dead, or any other person, including artists, models, police, and any place, or thing, is entirely coincidental and beyond the author's intent.

Visit the author's website at https://lisabuffaloe.com.

ISBN 978-1-957715-11-7 (eBook)
ISBN 978-1-957715-10-0 (Paperback)
ISBN 978-1-957715-12-4 (Hardcover)

Cover design: Lisa Buffaloe
Cover art photo of woman by Leeloo the first, used by permission.

Printed in the United States of America

To my Lord and Savior, Jesus Christ,
thank You for being the healer of the broken.

One
1965 – Eastern Europe

Defying darkness, moonlight slithered through frost-lined windows. Nika Selinsky waited and listened. Hoping no one watched, she slipped out of her cover; knelt on the cold, hard floor; and lifted the bottom leg of her bed. Reaching inside the hollow, black-metal tubing, she removed her treasures, the used papers, and pencils she'd taken from the schoolroom's trash bin.

In the quiet, she sketched distant memories from before her time in the orphanage—before her parents and younger brother died in the horrible car crash. Shivering, she closed her eyes and tried to tamp down the memory of the wreck, the explosion, the screams reverberating in her mind. She rubbed at the scar at the back of her head, the one no one could see because of her long hair. Yet, she would never forget.

Three years ago, the policeman had brought her here. Even now, she shuddered at the evil she'd seen in the heavyset man's dark-brown eyes.

Why had her uncle not come for her? Why had she been abandoned?

A cry came from the next bed as her friend, Denitsa, caught in another nightmare, her dark hair slick with sweat writhed in her sleep.

Nika rushed to hide her papers and supplies, then

touched her friend's arm, and kept her voice quiet. "Wake, it is only a dream."

Denitsa's eyes flew open. "Do not let them take me." Her voice whisper-strained in horror. "They will come, Nika." She gasped and clutched Nika's hand. "They will come."

"*No*. I will not let them take you."

Denitsa moaned and closed her eyes. "You will not be able to stop what will happen."

"No." Nika shook her head. "We will find a way." Yet, the horrible truth remained, Denitsa would be sixteen next month. The truck would soon come. No one knew where the girls were taken, only that they were never heard from again.

Footsteps sounded outside in the corridor. Nika and Denitsa scrambled under their covers. Keys jangled, the lock unlatched, and the door opened. Dim light from the hallway flickered across the dark floor.

A flashlight beam crossed each bed, pausing on Nika's face. Holding her breath, she forced her expression to remain calm and relaxed.

The door closed and muted voices of a man and woman came from the hallway as footsteps retreated.

Nika reached for her friend and squeezed her fingers. "Someday, we will escape."

Denitsa's tearful gaze met hers, then with a muffled cry, she rolled over to face the wall.

Staring at the dark ceiling, Nika willed herself to be brave. Her poppa always told her she must be strong, that fear was only an emotion to be ignored, and crying a sign of weakness.

She had to find a way to escape, but every door in

the orphanage stayed locked. The outside yard was surrounded by a brick wall with broken glass embedded on the top.

The only exit remained bolted except for deliveries and an occasional visitor.

Nika shuddered at the memory of the girl who had tried to escape. After she was captured, whatever they had done to her kept her from speaking for weeks. Her first response was only a scream. After that, the girl was taken away and never returned.

Two

Nika kept her back to the other girls as she gripped tightly her threadbare jacket and stared at the object in her friend's hands.

"You hold it like this," Denitsa whispered as she cradled a dirty cloth doll against her chest, then held it toward Nika. "Here, you try."

"No, I am too old to play with such things."

"You are only fifteen." Denitsa sighed and stroked the doll's matted hair. Dark circles lined her green eyes. Although a month older, she was smaller, tiny. She'd been here longer, brought to the orphanage when she was only seven. A long, faded scar ran along her cheekbone, marking the time she'd attempted to protect another girl from the headmistress's wrath.

"Dolls are for little girls." Nika tucked the musty gray blanket around her bed, making sure no creases remained.

"When we are older, do you think we will have babies?"

"No." Nika's stomach twisted and convulsed. "We must not." *No one else should live like this.*

"I want to have a baby." Denitsa's eyes met hers.

"Why?"

"To love and be loved." Denitsa clutched the doll to her chest, then grabbed Nika's hand. "Someday, we will have a good life. I dreamed I was with my momma, and she kept saying over and over that God loved me."

Nika recoiled. *God could not love them.*

"I had forgotten." Denitsa continued, her voice quiet. "Momma used to read from the Bible. When I was little, she told me about a boy who killed a giant, about people being chased by a bad army and then God opened a sea for them to escape. I had forgotten the stories, but now I remember. God will help us escape too."

Turning away, Nika shook her head. Her friend had such hope, but what use was hope in a place like this?

The bell rang, signaling the first meal. Footsteps scurried, echoing down the hall as the other girls rushed to the dining room.

After shoving the doll under her mattress, Denitsa made her bed.

"Girls!" The headmistress dressed in drab black, her black hair pulled back from her pale face, stood in the doorway and rapped her wooden rod against the wall. "Get going, or there will be no food for you."

The girls hurried past the woman.

Farther down the hall, Denitsa grabbed Nika's arm. "Did she see the doll?" Panic constricted her whisper.

"I do not think so." At least Nika hoped not. The last time someone had been found with an unauthorized toy, the girl had been given a beating that left her back bloody for weeks. Nika stepped closer to Denitsa, wishing she could shield and forever keep her friend safe.

Filing behind the others, they sat at the scratched and marred wooden dining table. No one spoke; no one made eye contact.

Nika stole a glance at the one clear window on the far wall. In the distance, hints of green showed in the trees on the hill. Beyond that, the city.

The girls stared straight ahead and waited for a small portion of food to be placed in front of them. A few of the girls received more, those who were the headmistress's favorites. The youngest, who had a chance to be taken by families, were preferred.

Nika and Denitsa were considered too old to be noticed by prospective parents who wanted babies or small children. Once they had reached the age of fourteen, their schoolwork had been replaced with chores, laundry, cooking, cleaning, and during the summer months tending the garden.

"Denitsa!" The headmistress stood at the end of the long table and held out the doll. "Is this yours?"

Wide-eyed, Denitsa choked on her food.

Before her friend could respond, Nika jumped to her feet. "It is mine."

The headmistress laser focused her with a stare. "Yours?" Her voice oozed disdain.

"Yes." Nika clenched her fists and locked her knees to keep them from trembling.

Denitsa's tear-rimmed eyes pleaded with Nika.

With her heart pounding, Nika faced the headmistress and raised her chin. "It is mine."

The woman's gaze turned to Denitsa, then she tore the head off the doll.

Grabbing Nika's arm, the woman squeezed with so much force, she fell to her knees. "Since you say the doll is yours, *you* will face punishment."

Three

Her legs weak, Nika swatted away the flies and then continued dicing potatoes barely fit for human consumption. She had survived a week locked in a cell in the freezing, dark basement with no blanket and no bed. A week without sunlight, with very little food and water, and only a bucket in the corner to relieve herself. A week throwing her few crumbs of moldy bread to keep a large rat at bay. Yet, she never cried. She would *never* give the headmistress the satisfaction of knowing she had been frightened.

"Why did you do such a thing? I heard the doll was not even yours," Andrea, the new woman working in the orphanage kitchen, said as she studied her.

"I will do anything to keep my friend safe."

Nika glanced her way. The woman's brown hair was pulled back from her face. Although her brown dress was faded, her shoes looked new.

"Interesting." Andrea's knife rhythmically chopped cabbage. "Perhaps at times, friendships could be a good thing." Her knife paused, her gaze resting on Nika. "Other times, those we consider friends can be used against us."

Nika turned back to her task and chopped faster and harder. Denitsa was all she had.

Yet no matter how she tried to protect her friend

from the headmistress, the clock continued ticking to their sixteenth birthdays. No parties would be given, only a terrible unknown.

Four

"**Y**ou are a beautiful girl. Not many have blonde hair with such interesting blue eyes." The headmistress's coal-black eyes surveyed Nika, then her gaze rested on Nika's chest. "You have developed nicely."

Throat tightening, Nika did not reply. She stood at attention in front of the headmistress's large, wooden desk. The office displayed nothing personal, only documents on the wall from the state certifying the headmistress had the right to run the orphanage.

From a row of metal file cabinets lining the back wall behind her desk, the woman retrieved a folder with Nika's name. Her leather chair squeaked as she sat and studied what was written in the folder. "You have done well with your studies. Your French is excellent; your English could use work." She motioned to the wood chair in front of her desk. "Sit."

Nika complied.

The woman rose, crossed to the door, then turned back. "You are to remain here." Stepping into the hallway, she locked the door behind her.

Minutes passed. Finally, Nika took a chance and walked to the window. A truck parked outside waited by the front door. Her knees weakened as dread rippled through her. Inhaling deep breaths, she willed herself to be strong.

Male voices came from the next office, followed by the sound of a struggle.

"*Niiiiiikkkkkkkaaaaaa!*" Denitsa's desperate cries echoed in the hallway.

Rushing to the door, Nika screamed. "*No!*" She flung herself against the solid wood, banging her body against it, trying desperately to break through. Bruised and unsuccessful, she ran to the window again to look outside. Nauseating heat gushed through her veins. She screamed as the men dragged Denitsa to the truck and tossed her inside. They locked the doors and drove away.

Five

Two terrible days had passed since they took Denitsa. Ramming her fists into her eyes, Nika refused to let the tears fall. It was her fault. She should have broken down the door or thrown a chair at the window, ran to the truck, and pulled her friend to safety. Staring at the empty mattress next to her, she fought the stomach-gripping fear of what might be happening.

Nika rocked on her bed. A rat scurried past her foot. She pulled her legs to her chest and locked her arms around them. She must get away. Maybe when she went outside to empty the waste from the kitchen, she could slip through the gate...if it was open for deliveries. Or perhaps she could pick the locks and escape in the night. She *had* to find a way.

Footsteps echoed in the hallway. The lock released, and the door opened.

Falling back on her bed, Nika sucked in a breath as a flashlight beam shone brightly on her face.

"Get dressed and come with me." The headmistress's stern voice froze Nika's heart.

With trembling hands, she dressed. No one in the dormitory made a sound. If anyone had awakened, they would dare not move.

The woman jerked her by the arm, then dragged and pushed her down the dimly lit hall.

Nika could barely keep her feet under her.

"Hurry," the headmistress growled.

Stopping at the front door, the woman turned to her. "You are friends with Denitsa, yes?"

Her muscles trembled, yet she refused to show fear. Nika raised her chin. "Yes."

The woman stepped closer, her coal-black eyes soulless. "Then you will do what is asked of you, or your friend will pay the price."

The front door opened, and a giant, muscular man leered at Nika. "We'll take her from here." He grabbed her and plunged a needle into her arm.

Six

Head swimming, Nika forced her eyes open and tried to focus in the dingy light. Her arms were numb. She tried to move her hands, but her wrists were bound tight against her back. Her heart hammered in her chest as she struggled on the cold, cement floor to free herself.

The door opened, and the giant of a man holding a camera stepped inside the room. His flat-black gaze roamed across her body as he moved closer.

"Awake? Good." He spoke in her native tongue with a raspy voice. "Afraid? You should be." His clothes reeking of cigarette smoke, he reached down and ran his hand across her face.

Heat rocketed through her body, and she tried to squirm away. A flash from his camera blinded her. She closed her eyes, writhing on the concrete floor.

"Yes, keep struggling. That is good." He took more photos, then stepped closer. His rank, tobacco breath churned her stomach. "Now, we move to the next phase." He grabbed her arm, forced her to stand, and pressed her body against his.

Rough, calloused hands held her tight in with one arm, while his other hand roamed over her body. "Shame they will not let me do what I want."

His laugh was dark and evil as he removed the

ropes binding her wrists, then dragged her out of the room and down a hallway. Unlocking a sturdy door, he pushed her inside another dark space. She shuddered at the sound of the rattling keys as he locked her inside.

In the corner, something moved, groaned, and moaned in pain. Fighting fear, Nika stepped forward. Green eyes surrounded by deep bruises gazed her way.

Nika's body went cold. "Denitsa?" Dropping to her knees, she gently wrapped her friend in her arms. "What did they do to you?"

Through swollen and bloody lips, a sobbing wail rose from deep inside her friend's throat. Nika held her tight, rocking her, her friend's cries tearing apart her heart.

The door opened, a bright overhead light flicked on, and the big man walked inside, followed by a blonde woman dressed in a red miniskirt and white boots.

"My name is Tatiana. You will both live with me and do what I tell you to do. Do you understand?"

Nika jumped to her feet, ready to tear into the evil woman. "What did you do to her?"

The man squeezed her arm in his vice-like grip and raised his fist.

"No!" Tatiana shoved him out of the way. "This one is *never* to be touched." She ran her hand along Nika's face. "We have other plans for her. Bring her to me." She turned and left.

Trying to shield Denitsa, Nika backed away from the big man. "I will not leave her."

"You have no choice, stupid girl." He jerked her toward him and fastened a blindfold over her eyes.

She stumbled forward as he led her up several flights of stairs and a long hallway. A door opened, and her blindfold was removed. Nika swallowed a gasp as she stood in a stately room with tall ceilings and modern, elaborate furnishings.

Tatiana lit a cigarette and pointed to a white couch. "Sit." She then directed her gaze at the man. "Leave us."

He nodded and closed the door behind him.

"Do you like?" Tatiana sat next to her. The woman's smile was reptilian. "This is where you will live from now on. Better than where you were, don't you think?"

Nika refused to answer.

"If you do as I say, you will have a comfortable life." Tatiana leaned toward her and blew smoke in her face. "If you do *not* do as I say, your friend will suffer the consequences."

Seven

"I am sorry. It will not open." Nika again pushed against the bolted-shut window, but no matter how hard she tried, she couldn't make it budge. She stared at the ground below. From this height, the fall would be painful, if not tragic. Still, she had to find a way out, a way to save her friend.

"Stop." Denitsa stood next to her. "You have apologized a million times, and you have tried over and over again to find a way out. It's not your fault we are here. At least we are together."

"Yes, but I wish it was different." A week had passed, and they remained locked in a bedroom on the far end of the third floor of wherever they had been taken. The room was better than the orphanage. Even though the bedding was stained, the two pink canopy twin beds and the two desks with chairs were nice. They even had a private bath. Decent meals had been served every day, and yet unseen darkness seemed to hover around them.

The lock on the door released and Tatiana stepped into the room. "I have brought you something to wear." She addressed Nika and held out a dress and shoes. "Put these on and come with me."

"Is she coming?" Nika pointed to her friend.

"No. She'll be fine." Tatiana walked to Denitsa,

rested her hand on her cheek, then turned to Nika, "as long as *you* do as I tell you."

Nika nodded and quickly dressed.

Once she was ready, Tatiana and the big man led her downstairs and stopped at a closed door.

"You will do exactly as the photographer tells you," Tatiana said. "You will not speak unless I tell you what to speak. If you say anything or do anything the photographer or I do not tell you to do, Denitsa will pay for your insubordination. She will be beaten. Do you understand?"

Nika fisted her hands and nodded.

"I am your agent. When you address me, you will call me Ms. Tatiana. Do you understand?"

"Yes."

"Good. You will only speak French today; do not use your native tongue. You are given an opportunity to make you and your friend's life better, but you must do exactly as I tell you."

Tatiana opened the door, and a man with jet-black hair stood alongside an older woman. The room was filled with lights and camera equipment.

The woman stepped forward and fingered Nika's hair, then addressed Tatiana. "Magnifique! She is the one." Taking Nika by the hand, the woman led her in front of a large white canvas drop cloth. "Stand here."

The man behind a camera took several photos as the woman adjusted Nika to stand straighter and tilt her head. "Yes, now smile."

Nika tried; she really did.

Tatiana came beside her and leaned down to whisper. "Smile, or there will be terrible consequences for your friend."

Nika imagined escaping far away from these evil people, then smiled her best.

"Yes! That's it," the woman said. "Ah, the innocence, yet with a touch of sadness. Tatiana, you have done well."

She then addressed Nika again. "Now, turn like this." She adjusted Nika to stick out her chest and throw her head back. The woman then moved her to different sets in the room to sit on a couch, then a chair, and to wear outfits that clung to her body and exposed more than she would ever choose to wear. Even her hairstyles were changed as they posed her in ways that made her sick to her stomach.

"Good. I have what we need today," the man said, addressing Tatiana. "We will return to continue once these are processed and sent to our customers."

"She will be ready." Tatiana smiled at the couple, then took Nika by the hand.

The big man waiting in the hall stepped toward them. "How did she do?"

"We have a natural. The true test will come soon."

Nika's skin crawled at the man's deep chuckle.

Back in their room, Denitsa ran to Nika as soon as the door closed behind her. "Are you okay? Did they hurt you?"

"No." Nika sat on her bed and hugged a pillow to her chest. "They took photos. Lots and lots of pictures."

"Tatiana and the man?"

"No. Another man and an older woman." Nika tried to stop the quiver in her voice. "They had me dress in different outfits and fixed my hair like you would see in a magazine. They did not hurt me, but they are scary."

"Oh, Nika." Denitsa's chin trembled as she sat next to her.

"They will take me back soon. I do not want to go."

Denitsa clung to her. "We must escape."

Nika hugged her friend tight then shoved off the bed and walked to the window. If only she could get it open. Maybe she could throw a chair and shatter the glass. She'd risk the fall for herself, but she wouldn't take the risk that Denitsa would be hurt.

Movement on the grounds outside drew her attention. A man pushed a wheelbarrow filled with flowers and yard equipment past the swimming pool. He stopped, scanning around him, then his gaze traveled to their window. Taking his shears, he cut off two flowers and held them against his chest. He nodded, smiled, then continued on the path leading behind the hedges.

Nika stepped back. "Did you see that?"

"Yes, what do you think that means?" Denitsa grabbed her arm.

"I do not know. But I think he knows we are here."

"Is that good? Do you think he is nice? Maybe he will rescue us."

Nika didn't reply. Perhaps the man was sending another message that they would be cut off like the flowers.

The door unlocked and Tatiana stepped inside, carrying a tray of food. "Dinner is served. Eat well." She placed the tray on Nika's desk.

The giant man followed behind with a basket of

bath products. "For the girls." Nika's stomach turned sour at the sight of his leering smile.

"You did well today." Tatiana placed her ice-cold hand on Nika's shoulder. "I have bubble baths and delicious oils for your skin. I want you both to use them."

After they left, Nika poked at her food. Dread pressed on her shoulders. She had to be brave and strong and do whatever was necessary to protect Denitsa. But who would protect her?

Eight

"Non, no, no. Like this." The photographer tilted Nika's head to the left. "These photos will be perfect for our needs. Put on your next outfit, and we'll move to the next portion of the shoot."

"Darling." Tatiana strolled toward her. "Make sure you pay attention. The man knows his business." She leaned closer, her hot breath against her ear as she spoke in Nika's native tongue. "Be good or there will be hell to pay."

Nika nodded. Under the older woman's supervision, Nika put on a tight, red shirt and shorts—the fabric cold and clingy against her skin. She shuddered. How could she escape these people? Maybe she could cut her hair, break her nose, or scar her face so they couldn't use her, then she could run far away with Denitsa to a place where they would never be found.

The door opened and a muscular young man, shirtless and wearing a pair of jean shorts, entered. "Are you ready for me?"

The photographer waved his hand. "Only a few more minutes. Wait in the other room."

"Nika, hurry. Take off those clothes." The older woman then pulled a nightgown that revealed way too much in the front and barely covered her in the back.

More photos were taken as she stood shivering.

"We have enough of these." The photographer said.

"Nika, darling. Come with me." Tatiana took her by the hand and led her down the hall.

When the door opened, the young man laid naked on a bed. She turned to run, but the giant's hands grabbed and held her fast.

Tatiana jerked Nika around and got in her face. "You will do *exactly* as you are told." Her voice hissed. "You know what will happen to your friend if you do not."

Nika's knees turned to water as they dragged her forward.

The man's lips curved in a sinister smile as he grabbed her hand. "Do not worry." He pulled her against his hot chest and held her tight. "I will take good care of you."

Mind crumbling, Nika squeezed shut her eyes and refused to watch what they did to her body.

Nine

Screams and curses from the hallway pulled Nika from the edge of consciousness.

The door splintered and shattered.

"Police!" Black masks covering their faces and carrying guns, they rushed into the room. The man who had done terrible things to her body yelled curses as he was dragged away. The other adults were handcuffed and shoved out of the room.

"You are safe now." A woman's voice came from beside Nika as a covering was laid across her bare shoulders. "Hurry, you must put on your clothes."

Shivering, engulfed in waves of nausea, Nika complied as the policewoman helped her dress.

Gentle hands led her through a hallway to a car parked behind the house. Sirens blared in the distance. Acrid smoke burned Nika's nostrils.

Wide-eyed, tears running down her face, Denitsa sat in the backseat and vaulted into her arms as she slid next to her.

Still masked, a policeman in the front seat turned as the policewoman slid into the passenger's seat beside him. "The film has been destroyed."

"Good." The woman turned toward Nika. "For your safety, you must lay down on the floorboards." The woman's voice was kind but urgent.

The car's engine roared, and tires squealed as the vehicle pulled away.

Nika glanced back at the house. Smoke and flames boiled out of the doorway. Swallowing the bile rising in her throat, she turned away. The fire would never be hot enough to burn away the hell she had endured.

A quilt was laid on top of them, enshrouding them in darkness. Sobbing, Denitsa laid against her as Nika held her close. No tears of her own came. Instead, she shoved what the people did to her into the recesses of her mind and locked them far away into a dark, soulless void. She could not, would not, *ever* speak of what had been done to her.

Ten

"**N**ika, Denitsa, you may sit up." The woman's voice came from the car's front seat. "It's safe now."

Blinking in the sunlight, they crawled out from under the cover and huddled together in the backseat. The car sat parked on the side of the road in the countryside.

Unmasked, the gardener they had seen outside the window at Tatiana's looked across the front seat at them. "I am Mikhail. Those at the orphanage, Tatiana, and the people associated with them will never hurt either of you again."

"I am Isabella." The woman, also maskless, smiled. "We are taking you to a safe house run by Gabrielle. She will take good care of you, help you finish your education, and receive any training necessary to start your lives when you are old enough."

"Why do you do this?" Nika sat straight. "Who is this woman? What happened to the other girls? Why only us?"

"The others have been taken where they will truly be cared for," Isabella said. "Because of your ages and a few other factors, you will live with Gabrielle."

Mikhail nodded. "When Gabrielle was younger, she also went through many difficulties. Now she helps girls like you. You will be safe. I trust her with my life."

Nika surveyed the man. Something in his eyes, the tone of his voice, made her trust him, but still...how could she ever be safe again?

"She is a wonderful woman and helped me when I was younger," Isabella added.

"What if we do not like this lady?" Nika grabbed Denitsa's hand. She had to keep her safe.

"We have written our phone numbers on the papers we will give you. You may call at any time, and we will come." Mikhail handed them documents. "For your safety, your names have been changed. You are now Veronika Zabelle and Deni Cadieux. It is most important you remember and always use your new names."

"Hello, Veronika." Deni/Denitsa grinned and shook her hand. "I told you God would rescue us."

"Hello, Deni." Veronika/Nika returned the handshake but did not smile. Perhaps God had saved her friend, but her rescue had come too late. She would never be the same again. Whatever happened next, she was only along for the ride.

As they traveled through the rolling countryside, Mikhail and Isabella talked quietly in the front seat. Traveling east, they passed through a small village with cobblestone roads. An old woman, her hair in a scarf and her brown coat tattered, trudged along the street. A man on a bicycle glared at them as they passed.

Nika studied the papers. Her new name now was Veronika Zabelle. *Veronika Zabelle.* She must remember. Yes, she could become someone new and leave Nika behind forever. She hunkered down in the seat as the car bumped and curved through villages and rolling countryside.

Deni leaned back and drifted off to sleep.

Hoping to at least rest, Veronika closed her eyes. But vivid scenes played in her mind.

She leaned down out of sight and clawed at her scalp, trying to purge the memories.

What happened to her must never come to light.

Eleven

"**G**irls, we're almost there." Isabella's voice held a note of excitement.

Veronika rubbed her tired eyes. They had traveled all night with Mikhail and Isabella taking turns at the wheel, often driving over roads that seemed more like dirt paths. Fortunately, Isabella had kept them well-fed throughout the trip. The stops they made for petrol were quick but had given them time to take care of their needs and stretch their legs.

Sunshine streamed through the car's window as they drove through a small village with stone houses and red tile roofs. A man, standing in the doorway of a market, smiled and waved as they passed.

Mikhail returned the greeting and continued driving for a few more minutes, then he turned the car and stopped at an iron gate set in a low, moss-covered stone wall. "We're here." He got out, stretched, then opened the gate before continuing the drive down a gravel road.

A large brown horse and two goats stared at them as they drove past. The car stopped in front of a two-story stone farmhouse with light blue shutters. An ivy-covered stone wall ran around the perimeter. Chickens scratched and pecked in the yard.

The front door opened, and a big, furry, white dog

bolted out, followed by a little blonde-haired girl in a simple, flowered dress. She smiled wide. "Momma G., they are here!"

An attractive woman with salt-and-pepper hair pulled back in a soft bun wore a white apron over a much-used, blue-cotton dress. She waved. "Bonjour. Hello, girls. Welcome."

As soon as Mikhail stepped out of the car, the woman wrapped her arms around him. "Son, it's good to see you."

His face reddened. "Oh, Momma."

"Did you have any trouble?"

"No, God was with us and granted us favor."

The dog jumped and wagged at Mikhail's feet. "Woof! Hey, boy." He rubbed the dog's fur as the animal danced around him.

Gabrielle turned to Isabella and placed her hands on either side of her face. "Dear one. How good it is to see you." The women embraced in a long hug.

Mikhail pointed to the girls. "Momma, this is Veronika Zabelle and Deni Cadieux."

Gabrielle held out her arms. "Welcome to my home."

The little girl stepped from behind Gabrielle. "I am Simone. We are glad you're here. And this is Woof." She pointed to the dog. "He won't hurt you. He is here to protect us."

Wagging his tail, the big dog sat at attention while his big brown eyes surveyed them.

"Come in." Gabrielle pointed to the house. "I will show you to your room. I made sure to keep you together since you are friends."

"You are across the hall from me." Simone smiled. "I'll show you around once you're settled."

The aroma of freshly baked bread, flagstone floors covered in warm rugs, and whitewashed stone walls covered in brightly colored paintings of flowers beckoned entrance into the living area.

Veronika stepped inside, pausing to note the location of doors and windows. A window in the back framed the outside overlooking a greenhouse and garden. To the right, the kitchen and dining area. Two floral couches sat in front of a stone fireplace flanked by shelves of books. A table on the far wall held photos of smiling girls and a plaque that read, *Veritas Vos Liberabit*.

Deni smiled at Veronika. "It is beautiful, no?"

"Yes, it is nice." She'd never seen anything as comfortable, cozy, and welcoming, but Tatiana had beautiful things and it was only a cover for horror and ugliness.

"Momma, G., may I show them to their room?" Simone asked.

The woman smiled and gave her head a gentle pat. "That would be nice. Thank you."

The little girl jumped in excitement and pointed up the stairs. "Come on. You will love your room. I helped get it ready for you."

Veronika and Deni followed her up wooden stairs and entered a room decorated in bright yellow, green, and orange florals on twin beds, with matching curtains hanging at the windows, and two wooden dressers.

"Momma G. bought you clothes. I hope you like them." Simone came close and took their hands in hers.

"This is a good place. I was brought here last year. You do not have to worry. We are safe. Come, I will show you our bathroom, the art room, and the study room."

Simone giggled as she showed them around. "It's wonderful here." She then pulled them outside on a flagstone patio ringed in pots of blooming flowers. "The plants stay pretty all year because Momma G. keeps them inside the greenhouse in the winter, and then when it is warm, we bring them outside. Sometimes we eat out here too."

"Girls, come back in. I have dinner ready," Gabrielle called from the doorway.

Following the others inside, Nika stood with them around a large circular wooden table. Two large loaves of fresh bread sat in the middle, along with a large serving bowl of soup. Veronika's stomach growled as she stood waiting unsure of what to do next.

"I will pray before we start the meal." Gabrielle folded her hands in front of her and bowed her head. The others did the same.

Veronika watched though, wondering what would happen.

"Dear Heavenly Father," Gabrielle said. "Thank you for bringing Veronika and Deni to this home you have given us. May they be happy and healthy here. Please bring comfort and healing. May they feel your joyful presence as they stay with us. Give them full tummies, sweet sleep, and much joy. We ask these things in the name of your Son, Jesus Christ, who is our Savior. Amen." Gabrielle lifted her head, smiled, and directed the girls to sit anywhere they would like at the table. "Girls, take as much as you want to eat; more is available in the kitchen."

During the meal, the adults talked and laughed, catching up with each other's lives.

Veronika ate as she listened to their easy banter. Would things change when Mikhail and Isabella left?

Once they finished, even the adults helped clean the table and wash dishes.

Mikhail wiped his hands on a dishtowel. "Momma, we must go." He hugged his mother and turned to Veronika and Deni. "You will be safe here. I will visit often."

"As will I." Isabella leaned down. "I lived here for five years, and it was the happiest time of my life. This place is special. Momma G. is special. Heal, grow, and enjoy the gift you have been given."

Gabrielle followed the policemen to the car. Huddling together, they talked in low tones.

Veronika leaned against the doorframe watching, looking for any clues as to what might happen next.

Gabrielle returned and smiled at her. "Now it's time to do a little reading before bedtime. Come, let's sit together on the couch."

Simone squealed and ran to the bookshelf next to the stone fireplace. "May I choose tonight?"

"Yes, dear. What would you like us to read?"

"This one!" Simone held out a brightly colored storybook.

"Ah, yes. This is one of my favorites."

Veronika sat spellbound as Gabrielle's voice rose and softened as she read a story of a knight, princess, and a dragon. The knight was brave, yet the princess was even braver as they fought together the dragon. As the last page was read, they sighed in unison at the happy ending.

"I love that story." Deni leaned her head back on the couch. "Thank you for reading to us."

Gabrielle closed the book and gazed at each of them. "Stories can lead us on adventures, and they can also teach us. They remind us that even though bad things happen, even though at times we must battle, we can be brave."

"I will fight the dragon!" Simone raised her hand as though carrying a sword.

"You, little one, have bravely fought all your life." Gabrielle turned to Veronika and Deni. "As have you two girls. Now, it's time for my brave princesses to get ready for bed. I'll be up soon to tuck you in and say our nighttime prayers."

Veronika followed Deni and Simone as they ran up the stairs. Soft, pink nightgowns had been laid on each bed, and on their pillows was a little handwritten card with the words, *You are loved.* Her eyes swam as she stared at the words. How could she be loved by someone who did not know her? How could *anyone* love her after what had been done to her? She shoved the note aside and got ready for bed.

A few minutes later, Simone stood in the doorway, dressed in a floor-length, pink nightgown. "I hope you sleep well."

Snuggling into their warm beds, Deni and Veronika waited.

Gabrielle hugged Simone as she walked into their room. "Come on, little one. You can join us in here, and then I'll tuck you in."

Simone bounded toward them and smiled shyly at Deni. "Can I sit on your bed?"

"Yes." Deni smiled and patted the covers.

Grinning, Simone perched on the edge.

"Girls, I know this is your first night, and everything is new and probably a little scary." Gabrielle knelt on the floor beside them. "The porch light will always stay on at night, and Woof sleeps downstairs to keep watch. He will never hurt you; he is our protector. My bedroom is down the hall if you need anything. Day or night, if you need *anything*, you come to get me or call out. The house is old and creaks at times, but this house was given to me by God to care for girls who need a safe home. Every inch of this house and property has been prayed over and offered to God for his service. You are safe here." She smiled like an angel at them, then bowed her head. "Heavenly Father, thank you again for bringing these precious girls into my care. Bless them, and please watch over them tonight as they sleep. Help them rest peacefully in your loving care. We look forward to tomorrow and spending time together. We love you, Father, and ask these things in the name of your Son, Jesus Christ, who is our Savior. Amen." She rose and kissed the forehead of each girl. "Sleep well. You are loved."

"Good night." Simone skipped to her room.

Gabrielle stopped at the doorway. "I'll leave on the lamp by your bed and the hall light. My door will stay open if you need anything. Do you have any questions for me before I go?"

Both girls shook their heads no.

"All right. Good night. I'll see you in the morning."

Gabrielle hummed as she left the room.

Deni turned toward her friend. "Nika. I mean, Veronika, could we move our beds together? Do you think she would mind?"

"I think it will be okay. We will be quiet." Veronika got out of bed and pushed hers close to Deni's. Reaching out toward her, they held hands.

"Are we finally safe?" Deni's gaze searched Veronika's face.

"I hope so."

"I hope so too." Deni squeezed Veronika's hand and closed her eyes.

Eyes wide open, Veronika listened to the quiet sounds of the house, keeping watch as her friend relaxed and drifted off to sleep. If she went to sleep, would this only be a dream?

Daring herself to close her eyes in the darkness, tormenting memories flashed in her mind. The man, the photographer, the others who had come into the room, the sickening reality that before the police arrived, terrible, awful, nightmarish things had happened to her. Flinging off her covers, she tiptoed to the bathroom and turned on the bathtub water.

Scrubbing and washing, she scratched at her skin and scalp, trying to rid herself of the memories that tortured her soul.

Twelve

"**G**ood morning!" Already dressed for the day, Simone jostled them awake, bouncing on their beds, and tugged on their arms. "Let's go feed the animals while Momma G. makes breakfast."

Sleep morphed into awareness. The sun barely peeked over the horizon; Veronika tried to focus.

Deni jumped to her feet and tugged the covers off Veronika. "Come on, sleepyhead. I smell food."

"Ugh." Her traitorous mouth watered at the yummy fragrance coming from downstairs. She stumbled out of bed and looked for her clothes.

Simone pointed. "Momma G. put everything in your dressers for you last night."

"She did?" Veronika rubbed her eyes. Maybe she *had* been able to sleep. Stepping closer, she pulled a drawer open and looked inside. Sure enough, cute clothes in her size were arranged in the drawers. Fingering the items, she couldn't believe someone would know what she would like to wear. No one had bought her anything since her Momma had died. She fisted her hands and rubbed the moisture from her eyes.

"Momma G. always stays up late to make sure we sleep well. I will meet you downstairs." Simone skipped out of the room.

Deni squealed as she held up a new outfit she found in her dresser. "Look at this! Is it not perfect?"

Veronika nodded and found herself a cute top and pants. For now, everything seemed good, but even Tatiana had kept them in a nice room and had nice clothes to wear...for a while.

After dressing, they went downstairs.

Gabrielle, standing at the stove, turned toward them. "Good morning. Your breakfast will be ready when you finish your chores."

"Come on. I'll show you the way." Simone took their hands and tugged them outside.

As though on patrol, the big dog bounded next to them, wagging his busy tail and staying in step.

"We have chickens, two goats, a horse, and Bossy the cow." Simone bounced with her words as she led them to a stone building she referred to as the barn. She handed them a basket and pointed. "You can gather the eggs in the hen house while I milk Bossy. The chickens may make a little fuss, but they know that is their job. We feed them, and they feed us. Watch out for the little chicks. Momma G. will sell those to Monsieur Mathias."

Veronika followed Deni to where the chickens were kept. Sidestepping the baby chicks, she surveyed the nesting boxes. Several chickens clucked and stared at them.

Deni giggled as she reached under a chicken and pulled out two brown eggs. "Look! Isn't this fun?"

When one chicken squawked at Veronika, she stepped aside to let her friend continue to have the pleasure of removing any remaining eggs. Once their chores were completed, they hurried back to the house.

The table already set, Gabrielle took from them the eggs and the bucket of milk. "Wonderful job, girls. I am proud of you. Sit, let's pray, and enjoy the bounty the Lord has given us."

After breakfast, they all helped clean the kitchen. Gabrielle then led them into a bright, window-lined room with a small table and chairs for each girl. Once they were settled, she questioned Veronika and Deni on what they already had learned and the subjects they needed to continue their education. After that, Gabrielle then guided them around the property and explained about the land she owned and those who lived around them. Woof ran ahead as though checking to ensure everything was safe, then he would return and stay close. Simone patted him on the head and kept her hand on his furry back as they continued to stroll through a field.

Deni moved close and squeezed Veronika's arm. "This is all so wonderful."

"It is pretty." A few years ago, she would have been thrilled. Now, it was too late to enjoy the beauty that surrounded her.

Gabrielle stopped and pointed to a vineyard on a distant hill beyond trees. "Most of our neighbors are very nice. However, it is best that you do not go near the vineyard. They hire many people I do not know during harvest time."

Veronika surveyed the rolling hills, trees, and the vineyard in the distance. The area was beautiful and looked like something on a postcard.

When they arrived back at the house, Gabrielle

took the girls to the classroom and set a blank canvas and watercolor paints in front of each girl.

"Veronika loves to draw," Deni said.

"Is that right?" Gabrielle turned to Veronika. At her nod, Gabrielle removed a sketch pad and pencils from her desk and brought them to her. "You may enjoy these. Keep them; they are yours."

Veronika held them against her chest, relishing the feel of a new pad and pencil. She wouldn't need to scrounge for supplies.

Gabrielle then showed them step-by-step how to paint a flower, even letting them decide the colors to make it their own.

Using bright colors, Veronika let her brush play freely on the canvas. She glanced at what the other two girls were working on. Even though they each followed the same pattern, their paintings had unique aspects.

After dinner, Veronika curled onto the couch with the other girls and became engrossed in another tale of adventure and intrigue. Gabrielle then read from the Bible about the rescue of the people of Israel from the Egyptians and how God opened the Red Sea for them to cross.

After Gabrielle closed the book, her sweet gaze rested on them. "You have all been through difficult, hard, and tragic experiences. But always remember you made it through. God opened the way for you to make it to the other side. You, my little ones, are warrior princesses. Your life has meaning and purpose. God loves each of you and has a good plan for you. Never, ever forget that you are loved by God. Life isn't easy. Bad things happen, but remember, no amount of pain is wasted. Good things are coming and will come." She stood, walked to the bookshelves, and handed Veronika and Deni a Bible. "I have a gift for each of you. Simone already has a copy; these are for you to keep. The Bible is God's love letter to you. Read it often so you can get to know God and know better his love for you."

Deni hugged it to her chest. "Thank you. I will cherish it forever."

Veronika thanked her and flipped through the stiff pages. Why would she read the book from a god who had shown that she was not loved? If you love someone, you do not allow them to suffer.

* * *

Screaming, flailing, Veronika fought as demon hands gripped her tight, pulling her down, down, into the darkness. Jolting awake, she gasped for air, tossed off her covers, then stood quivering next to her bed.

Throwing on her robe, she clutched it tight around her body, and willed herself to focus on her surroundings. Early morning sunshine cast the neat and tidy room in an orange glow. Deni slept peacefully in her bed. The scent of baking bread and soft voices came from downstairs. Steadying herself, Veronika padded downstairs in her bare feet. Simone and Gabrielle were already busy baking. Still shaking from her nightmare, Veronika sat in the other room and watched them.

Gabrielle turned to Simone. "How many centiliters are needed?"

"Twenty-five," the little girl responded.

"Good. Now, how many cups would be in 480 milliliters?"

"Two."

"Good! Your math skills are excellent. Now let's check the oven and see how your creation turned out."

Simone took out a pan of rolls. "No. No. This is not good!" She stamped her feet and dropped the pan on the table. "I am a failure."

"No, failing at something does not mean you are a failure." Voice gentle and soothing, Gabrielle laid her hand on the little girl's shoulder. "Learning is a process for all of us. This may not have turned out as you planned, but they will taste good. Let's see what can be done differently as we work on the next batch."

Veronika sighed at the memories of her own mother's soft voice and touch. Why couldn't the past be changed and life be different? She would always be an orphan and always broken.

She padded upstairs, crawled into bed, and threw the covers over her head.

Thirteen

Schoolwork completed, Veronika carried her drawing supplies outside and climbed the hill closest to the house. Relaxing against a tree trunk, she sat, watched, and listened to the sounds of nature. How she had missed being outside. Spring's vibrant greens tinted the trees, and wildflowers swayed in a gentle breeze.

In a branch above, a yellow-breasted bird sang a tune worthy of an opera. Another bird in the distance twilled and chirped. As though on an important mission, bees buzzed past. Woof, the warrior dog, trotted up the hill, wagged his tail a few times, then sat a few feet from her, keeping watch.

Taking her pencil, she sketched the scene as sunshine warmed her face. The day reminded her of a weekend outing she had years ago with her family. She and her brother had played in a small creek while her parents relaxed nearby on a blanket. The day had been perfect, filled with joy and laughter, but everything changed the following week when their car was hit head-on by a truck.

Why did she survive? Veronika scratched and scrawled over her drawing. Today's beauty could never erase the ugliness of her past.

"What you doing?" Head cocked to one side, Deni stood over her.

Veronika closed her sketchpad. "Nothing."

"Can I see? I always love your drawings." Before she could stop her, Deni took the pad out of her hands and flipped it open. "This was beautiful. Why did you ruin it?"

Veronika frowned and crossed her arms. "I do not know."

Her friend sat next to her and handed back the pad. "I am sorry."

"For what?"

"For the things that make you mad and sad."

"It is not your fault."

"I am still sorry." Deni leaned against the tree, her shoulder touching Veronika's.

Silence lingered as a bumblebee flitted and landed on a pink wildflower nearby.

Veronika studied the insect. "My poppa would say bees look like they are wearing black-and-yellow vests."

Deni giggled. "I think that one's vest is too tight."

"Perhaps he is gathering pollen so he can court the queen."

"Yes, and then he would become king of the bee knights of the round hive." Deni giggled. "I wonder, if we could see across the field, would all the bees dance as they collected pollen for their hive? Would you draw a picture of that? Please?"

Veronika nodded and flipped open her sketchpad. As Deni interjected fun ideas and dialogue for the bees, Veronika drew pages and pages of a magical world of dancing bees and the brave bee knights of the round hive.

"Hello!" Simone skipped up the hill and sat next to them. "What you doing?"

"We are writing a book about bees," Deni said.

"I love bees, except when bees sting. Is the story about good bees?"

"Yes, but a bad bee will try to steal the queen." Veronika held up her drawing.

Simone put her hands on her mouth. "Oh, no. I do not like that kind of bee."

"Have no fear. Sir Lancebeelot will save the day."

"Yay! Will you take the book to Momma G. to read?"

"Yes, she will," Deni said. "We must share the story. Little bees around the world need to know of the brave bees of the round hive."

Simone moved closer. "Will little bees need protection in your story?"

Veronika nodded. "Yes, we will add little bees."

"Could two of them be named Bee kind and Bee good?"

Deni chuckled. "Yes, we could also have Bee brave and Bee mighty. Bee mighty could even be a super-big bee."

Veronika sketched the scenes as her friends gave her ideas and helped with the storyline.

"Girls!" Gabrielle's voice carried from the back patio. "Dinner is ready!"

"Come. We must go." Veronika closed her pad. "Last one to the house is a honey less bee."

Simone raced in front of them and shouted. "Momma G., we are coming!"

Panting from the race, they ran inside and gathered

around the table set with bread and a creamy chicken dish.

Gabrielle smiled. "I would have called you earlier, but you looked like you were having fun."

"We were!" Simone said. "Veronika is writing a book."

"Really?" Gabrielle laid a gentle hand on Veronika's shoulder. "Would you be willing to let me see after we eat this evening?"

Veronika nodded.

"Good."

After dinner, they sat at the table as Gabrielle studied what Veronika had drawn. "This is wonderful."

"Deni gave me the ideas for what the bees say," Veronika said.

"Girls, truly this is a very, very good book. The dialogue is great, and the drawings are excellent. I'm proud of you all for working together."

"Tomorrow, we will work again on the book." Veronika glanced at her friends. "Yes?"

Simone clapped. "I will beeee so happy."

Deni rested a finger against her chin. "To be or not to be, that is the question."

"You girls are fun. I will beeee anxiously waiting to see what you do next," Gabrielle said. "All of you are very intelligent with your schoolwork, and I am here for any area in which you might need help or anything else you'd like to learn."

"Will you help me with my writing?" Deni asked. "And I would also like to learn about business."

"Yes, those are good subjects to know. I will be glad to help."

"Will you help me bake that recipe you showed me the other day?" Simone asked.

Gabrielle nodded. "Yes, we can work on that this week."

"I would like to learn more about art." Veronika said.

"I'll be glad to teach you."

Veronika relaxed in her chair. Maybe, just maybe, her life finally had some hope.

* * *

The next afternoon after schoolwork was complete, she swirled her brush in the water and viewed the painting she was working on.

"Very good. The more water you use, the more translucent." Gabrielle's voice came from behind her. "If you use too much water, blot it gently with your rag."

Veronika nodded. "How do I paint a peony?"

"Use a small brush and make a shape like a letter c where you want to place the flower. Then, make the c bigger as you extend out from the center." Gabrielle spent the next hour teaching ways that made Veronika's picture seem alive.

She followed Gabrielle's directions as she crafted flowers in a world with sunny skies and beauty. Now, if only she could erase her past, jump into her painting, and start a new life.

Fourteen

Two weeks had passed, and Veronika sat with the other girls in the schoolroom.

Gabrielle opened a cupboard behind her desk, removed a clay pot, and dropped it on the floor. The pot shattered. The girl's mouths opened wide in shock.

"This pot did nothing wrong," Gabrielle said, "yet here it is broken on the floor. What happened to each of you was not your fault. Never forget that. You were not to blame."

Veronika stared at the pottery shards on the floor. It did not matter who was to blame; broken pieces could never be repaired.

"Now, what should I do with this broken pottery?" As though reading her mind, Gabrielle continued. "Should I throw it out?"

"Yes, why keep something broken." Veronika said.

"What happens if I don't pick up the pieces and leave them scattered on the floor?"

"Our feet might get cut on the broken pieces," Deni said.

"True. However, there is another option." Gabrielle removed from the cupboard a bright blue piece of pottery interlaced with gold. "Kintsugi is the Japanese art of repairing broken pottery with lacquer mixed with powdered gold, silver, or platinum. Notice how it now glows with beauty."

She held the pot out toward them. "When you take your broken pieces, your shattered heart to God, his restoration glows through with his healing. God's mending and renewal weaves a golden bond as the goodness of God binds and heals our wounds."

Gabrielle stooped to pick up the pieces and placed them on her desk. "If the brokenness in our lives is ignored and not taken to God, those areas will result in shards that cut the broken one and those around them." She paused and gazed at each girl. "You have all been through terrible things. You can ignore what happened or try to tough it out but refusing to deal with the past results in unhealed brokenness. However, you can become a shining one, a glowing one, by allowing God to heal your wounds. Nothing is too hard for him, no life is too shattered for God, and nothing is impossible for God. Allow his healing, light-filled restoration to shine in you and through you. For through the broken, God's light shines."

Veronika swallowed back the emotion rising in her throat. What would Gabrielle know about being broken? Had she lost her family? Had terrible things happened to her? Talk was cheap when life was easy. Crossing her arms over her chest, Veronika stared at the broken pieces on the floor. If God was all-powerful, then he could have stopped what happened to her.

That night, unable to sleep, Veronika rubbed her bleary eyes and tiptoed out of the room. A soft light came from the end of the hallway. Veronika drew closer and peered inside the partially open door as Gabrielle, facing away, pulled off her dress.

To stifle her gasp, Veronika put her hand over her mouth. Gabrielle's back was covered in long scars.

Putting on her nightgown, the woman knelt by her bed and prayed out loud. "Heavenly Father, thank you for another day. Thank you for always being such a good father. Thank you for Veronika, Deni, and Simone. Help them heal, grow, and feel your joyful, loving presence. Guide and grant me wisdom to love the girls with your love and take good care of them. Grant us all to sleep well tonight and prepare us for our day tomorrow. I love you, Father. And I ask these things in the name of your Son, Jesus Christ. Amen."

Veronika shook her head. With a scar-covered back, how could Gabrielle be thankful to God? Turning to go, the floor creaked under Veronika's weight. She froze in place.

"Veronika?" Gabrielle moved toward her. "Are you okay?"

"Yes. I could not sleep."

"I understand. Would you like to come in and talk?"

Veronika nodded and followed Gabrielle to two white fabric chairs in front of a big window.

"Have a seat." Gabrielle's smile was gentle as she put on her robe. "Would you like a blanket?"

At Veronika's nod, Gabrielle tucked a lightweight cover around her shoulders.

"I saw your back." Veronika sat and stared at the wooden floor bearing scars from years of use.

"I see." Gabrielle settled across from her. "I experienced some difficulty when I was younger."

"May I ask what happened?"

"My parents were not nice people. When I was

thirteen, I ran away from home. Unfortunately, I met even worse people."

"I am sorry," Veronika swallowed hard and pulled the blanket tighter around her shoulders.

"Thank you, dear. I was set free by soldiers who liberated that town. Two months later, I had Mikhail. Veronika, with God's help, sometimes what looks like the worst thing will turn into something good. My precious son, Mikhail, is a Godsend. Now, Mikhail's always watching for ways to help other children. And when Isabella was twelve, the police found her in an alley. She had been beaten and abused. Now, as an officer, she also looks for ways to help others." Gabrielle paused. "Life is hard, and people can do terrible things. God helps us through hardships and heals our broken places like that pottery I showed you. Scars might remain, but as God comforts and heals us, we can comfort others and be part of their healing."

Veronika rubbed her eyes. Maybe God healed Gabrielle, but how did anyone heal from what she had gone through? Her scars might not be visible, but nothing could erase what was taken from her.

"I am praying for you." Gabrielle laid her hand on her shoulder.

"Thank you." It was all Veronika could think to say. She rose to her feet, hurried to her room, and crawled into bed. Closing her eyes, she slept and dreamed of shattered and broken pots. She jerked upright at a sound and tried to focus. *Where am I?* As though stepping out of a fog, she took in her surroundings.

Across from her bed, Gabrielle held tight to Deni. "It's okay. I'm here." She rocked her sweat-drenched friend in her arms. "It was only a dream. You are safe."

Veronika stayed quiet, watching as Deni relaxed nestled against Gabrielle as she talked in soothing tones to her friend.

Deni sighed. "I am okay now. Thank you."

Gabrielle gently laid her in bed and covered her up. "You know I am always here for you girls."

"Thank you."

"Are you sure you'll be okay?"

"I think so."

Gabrielle turned to Veronika. "How are you doing?"

"I am okay," she snapped.

Gabrielle knelt by her bed. "Do you need a hug?"

"No."

Leaning close, Gabrielle kissed Veronika on the forehead. "Sometimes being brave means admitting you need help. You do not have to be strong all the time."

Veronika rolled over in her bed and faced the wall. She could not ever be weak; she had to be strong. If she broke further, nothing could ever put her back together again.

Fifteen

After the table was cleared, and the last dish washed and dried, Veronika hung the dishtowel over the sink edge. Simone and Deni had chatted away as they helped.

Gabrielle stood by the back door. "Instead of sitting in the classroom, we're going on a field trip, and then we will work on various art projects. Make sure you take a bathroom break, put on your most comfortable shoes, and meet me on the outside patio."

The girls hurried to get ready and gathered outside.

Gabrielle smiled at each of them. "First stop is the woods."

Woof strutted in front of them as though responsible for their protection as Gabrielle led them through the countryside into a grove of trees. Sunshine filtered through the leaves, and a light breeze tousled Veronika's hair. Woof let out what sounded like an irritated bark followed by a slight growl as he glared at a squirrel chattering in the branches above.

Gabrielle stopped in front of a large tree. "A few years ago, this was hit by lightning." She laid her hand on the blackened bark. "We all have scars, sweet ones. Some are external like this tree, and some are internal. The lightning left the tree wounded and vulnerable to pests and disease, but the tree refused to give up. She stretched her limbs upward to the sky, letting the sun bring healing to the wound and rain nourish its branches and roots. The scar remains but is now a badge of courage and a story of survival."

Veronika ran her hand along the dark gash in the bark. Maybe the tree had survived, but what remained was an ugly reminder of what happened.

"Come." Gabrielle led them back through the trees and down the hill.

Simone skipped next to Gabrielle with Woof by her side, followed by Deni.

Wishing she could just sit and sketch, Veronika lagged behind. The breeze caressed her face, and in the distance a bird called. A gray dove settled in the grass to her right and let out a soft coo. Even though her life had stopped, life went on around her.

Gabrielle continued toward the house, then stopped inside the greenhouse. She laid out seeds on the potting bench. "What do you notice about these?"

"They are brown and not very big," Simone said.

"Good." Gabrielle picked them up in her hands. "Are these seeds alive?"

Veronika shrugged. "No, and yes?"

"Correct. They are dead now, but once planted and given nourishment through the soil, water, and sunshine, they will produce life. One tiny seed can yield a mighty harvest." She took a seed and planted it in a clay pot already prepared with soil. "When our dreams seem to die, or something terrible happens, always remember that life resurrects from death." She paused and smiled. "There is always hope. Come. I want to show you something in the art room."

They followed and gathered around Gabrielle as she plopped a lump of clay on her desk. "A verse in the Bible, Isaiah 64:8, says God is the potter, and we are the clay." She grinned as she kneaded the reddish lump. "If I were the clay, I would not be happy at someone squishing and squeezing, trying to mold me. Ouch." Her voice went up an octave. "Whimper. Noooo. Ouch. Ouch. Ouch!"

Simone and Deni giggled as Gabrielle kept making funny noises.

"But the thing is," their guardian continued, "this piece of clay always wanted to be a gorgeous vase sitting in a grand castle." She stopped and picked up the clay and moved it to the windowsill. "What if I left it here in the sun?"

"It would get hard or crack," Deni said. "Or it would stay a lump."

Gabrielle nodded. "What if the clay refused to let me work with it?"

"It would always be a lump," Veronika said.

Gabrielle picked up the clay and placed it on a potter's wheel next to her desk. "To become a work of art, there is a process, and sometimes that process is painful." As the wheel turned, she worked with the clay, molding and forming it. The clay rose and changed until it became a beautiful vase, its curves elegant. "Now, when I take this to the furnace, fire it to be hardened, and paint it whatever color I desire, what was once only a lump of clay will be classified as a work of art."

Gabrielle wiped her hands on a rag. "Come." She motioned them to follow as she led them to the shed attached to the back of the barn. Inside, on top of an old wooden table, sat a hammer and sheets of various colored glass. She waited until they gathered around her. "Is this glass pretty?"

"Yes," Deni said. The other girls agreed, even Veronika.

"What would happen if I broke these with my hammer?" Gabrielle asked.

"They would be useless," Veronika said. "Trash."

"Are you sure?" Gabrielle moved the glass into a wooden box. "Would you all step outside for a moment, please?" Once they were outside the shed, she took the hammer and smashed the glass. "You can come back in. Now, let me show you what we can do with the broken pieces."

Simone grinned. "You could make a mosaic."

"Yes, or I could make stained glass. What was broken becomes a work of art."

"It was still broken," Veronika crossed her arms.

"True, but the artist doesn't see broken; the artist sees what it will become." Gabrielle paused and then motioned to the girls. "Please come with me."

They followed her out to the field. Stopping at the fence, she whistled. The big brown horse ran and stopped in front of her. "This is Beauty. Years ago, this mare was brought to me by a local farmer because the horse was wild, and no one could ride her or use her for anything. She needed to be broken. That sounds painful, but that is only the name given for the process of training and working with a horse to behave well, be able to carry a rider, pull a vehicle, and follow the directions of its trainer. As you've seen in pottery, stained glass, and mosaics, and with horses, brokenness can lead to much beauty." She rubbed and nuzzled the horse's nose.

As the other girls patted the horse, Veronika turned away. Keeping her head down, she tromped up the hill.

Deni caught up with her. "You are so quiet. Is everything all right?"

"Why can we not have one day, one stinking day, without Gabrielle giving us stupid object lessons and Bible stories." Veronika plopped on the ground and leaned her back against the tree.

Deni sat next to her. "I like what Momma G. shares."

"She is *not* your Momma."

"No." Deni's eyes shined with unshed tears. "She is not, but Momma G. loves me and loves you."

"She treats us nice and feeds us. What does that have to do with love?"

"That's part of love, isn't it?"

"Maybe." Veronika stared at the grass and then turned to Deni. "Why does Gabrielle keep lecturing us about being broken? Is she saying God broke us to make us into something else—something beautiful?" She said the last in a sarcastic voice.

"I don't think that's what she meant."

"Then what? We weren't beautiful until we were broken?" Veronika spat the words. "We aren't beautiful until God squeezes and molds us into something else? Is Gabrielle saying the only way I can be useful and beautiful is by being smashed to pieces?"

"No, I think she was telling us that even though we have been through bad things that God can help us heal and put us back together."

"If God was a loving God he would *not* have made us go through what we went through!"

Deni chewed on her fingernails. "I don't understand why, but I do believe God loves us."

Veronika shook her head. She loved Deni and did everything in her power to keep her safe. If God loved them, he would have kept them safe.

"Momma G. told me as long as the past stays bottled up, it will not heal," Deni said. "So, I guess talking about things helps."

"I do not care *what* she says."

Deni's mouth opened then shut.

"What?" Veronika turned to Deni. "Why are you staring at me?"

"You never told me what happened and never asked what happened to me."

"I do *not* want to tell, and I do not want to know." Veronika put her face in her hands. "I continue to have nightmares. I do not sleep well." She dropped her hands and stared at her friend. "I hate what happened to me. I hate whatever happened to you. I cannot fix anything, and I hate that we cannot change our lives."

"I don't want you to fix me. I just wanted you to listen..." Deni's words trailed off, her eyes shiny with tears.

Veronika swallowed hard, forcing the tears to stop that threatened to break free. "It would destroy me to know."

Tears streaming down her face, Deni turned away, then looked back. "We have *all* been through horrible things, but I want to go forward. I want you to go forward. Gabrielle told me we can get over our brokenness. We can heal."

"Maybe you can. I *cannot*." Veronika rose to her feet and stomped away.

Sixteen

When the morning sun barely shone over the horizon, Veronika trudged to the henhouse and approached Deni. "Sorry I am late. My stomach was upset."

Her friend turned away and didn't respond.

Veronika reached under a chicken to check for eggs, but it pecked her finger. "Ouch." Growling, she turned away. No matter what she tried to do, she didn't do anything right. She'd hurt her friend, and now she couldn't even get a stupid egg from a stupid chicken. She ran away into the barn and kicked at the hay.

Dust particles swirled in the sunlight filtering through the small window on the side of the barn. She wandered to where the farm implements—shovels, a hoe, and an old rusty milk bucket—were stored. Moving aside an old blanket, she stared at a weathered wooden crate. The chickens couldn't peck at them if they were locked away. She dragged out the crate and carried it toward Simone. "Look what I found. We can lock them up."

Eyes wild, Simone scrambled to her feet. Shaking, she backed away, and with a scream, she ran toward the trees. Woof followed behind her at full speed.

Deni dashed around the corner. "Get Gabrielle." She ran after the little girl.

Yelling for help, Veronika sprinted to the house.

Wiping her hands on a towel, Gabrielle rushed toward her. "What's wrong?"

"It is Simone." Veronika pointed. "She ran to the woods."

"What happened?" Gabrielle dropped the towel and ran next to Veronika.

"I found a crate to put the chickens in so they would not peck at us."

"We must hurry." Tears streamed down Gabrielle's cheeks as she yelled Simone's name and ran toward where the girl had gone.

When they got closer, Woof bounded toward them, barked, then turned and ran back into the woods. Running behind him, the big dog led them to where Simone, curled into a ball, was hiding under a bunch of wild shrubs.

Gabrielle knelt and gently cradled Simone against her chest. "It's all right, my darling. You are safe. I'm here, little one. You are safe." Still in tears, Gabrielle carried Simone back to the house and up to her room.

Deni collapsed on the couch with a dazed expression.

Veronika paced back and forth. Did she do or say something that caused the little girl's reaction? Of course, she did, but she didn't know what.

After what seemed like forever, Gabrielle joined them downstairs. "Simone is asleep, but I will go back and stay with her until she wakes." She sat on the couch. "Simone does not have scars on her outer body, but inside she has deep wounds. When she was small, some terrible people kept her locked in a wooden crate."

Veronika gasped. "I am sorry. I did not know." Shaking, she swallowed the bile rising in her throat as flashes of her time locked in the basement cell ran through her mind.

"I know you didn't have any idea." Although she stood next to her, Gabrielle's calm voice seemed far away. "When we go through traumatic events, sometimes things we see, hear, or even smell can trigger an unexpected response." She gently patted Veronika's shoulder. "That will get better with God's help, time, and love. For now, I will stay with Simone until she awakens."

Gabrielle returned upstairs as Deni followed.

Memories tormented and tumbled through Veronika's mind. Catching her breath, she ran to the kitchen and grabbed some matches. Hurrying outside, she ran to the barn and dragged the crate out into the open. Screaming, she stomped and smashed her foot through the boards. She stomped those who had hurt Simone. Stomped the headmistress, Tatiana, the photographer, and the men who did terrible things to her and Deni. She did not stop until the crate was destroyed.

Bending over, she heaved in air and stared at the remnants of the shattered crate. How would she explain to Gabrielle what she'd done?

Hoping no one was watching, Veronika gathered the wood fragments, took them to the burn barrel, placed hay on top, and set the remains on fire. A gust of air whooshed through the fire, pushing flying embers around her head. She stood her ground as smoke and ashes engulfed her. If only she could burn away all that had happened to her, to Deni, and to Simone.

The next morning, Veronika rubbed her forehead as she walked down the stairs. Sleep had eluded her, and now she had a nagging headache. Last night during dinner, she had apologized to Simone. But how do you apologize for shoving someone into a tormenting memory? Words did not seem adequate. Although things between them seemed better, a heaviness remained.

Veronika stopped at the bottom of the stairs.

Gabrielle's back was to her as she talked on the phone. "Would you bring an empty crate when you come tomorrow?" A pause. "Yes, I did have one, but I will pay extra if you would allow us to put the chickens in yours." Another pause. "Thank you. We will see you in the morning."

Veronika sucked in a breath and stepped toward Gabrielle. "I am sorry I destroyed your crate."

"Do not worry." With a gentle touch, she placed her warm hand on her face. "It is best we do not have one here for now. When Monsieur Mathias comes, will you help him gather the baby chicks?"

"Yes, I would like to help."

"Good. Thank you. I will have Simone stay with me when he arrives." She paused, her smile gentle. "You can trust Monsieur Mathias. He is a good man."

Veronika nodded and breathed in courage. At the sound of Simone and Deni coming down the stairs, she turned to face her friends. "Good morning."

"Morning," Deni said.

"Morning," Simone mumbled, looked down, but

glanced back up. Dark circles lined the little girl's eyes.

Gabrielle placed her arm across Simone's shoulder. "I have already taken care of Bossy, and Deni took care of the eggs. After we eat, would you help me with a baking project? I have a new recipe and would love your help."

Simone brightened. "I would like that."

During breakfast, Veronika picked at her food. She stole glances at Simone to make sure she was okay. The little girl did eat but left some food untouched on her plate.

After a quiet breakfast, everyone pitched in to help with cleanup.

Woof barked at the sound of a truck engine outside.

Gabrielle wiped her hands on her apron. "Monsieur Mathias has arrived. Veronika and Deni, would you be so kind as to help him? Simone, let's work our baking project."

While Gabrielle kept Simone's attention toward the kitchen, the other girls scrambled outside as an old green truck pulled aside the barn and stopped. Woof, wagging his bushy tail rapid-fire, stood by the vehicle.

Easing out of the truck, an older gentleman, wearing a well-worn beret and coat, patted Woof on the head, then turned toward them. "Bonjour. Did Gabrielle tell you I was coming?"

"Yes." Veronika stayed at a safe distance.

"Good." He removed his beret and placed it over his heart. "You will be my helpers this morning?" His kind, gray eyes surveyed them.

They both nodded.

"Wonderful. How many little ones does she have

for me?" He removed a crate from his truck and ambled toward the henhouse.

"I think we have twenty," Deni said.

"Good." He stopped and turned to them. "Would you prefer I stay near my truck while you work?"

Although his eyes and smile were kind, Veronika nodded. "It might be a little crowded if we all went inside."

"Yes, I thought so. But if you need help, please let me know." He laid the crate on the ground and stepped back. "I will take in the food supplies I brought to Gabrielle."

After he walked away, Veronika maneuvered the big crate into the chicken house.

"He is kind," Deni said, as she followed her friend inside and shut the door behind her.

"Yes, I think so. So, how do we do this?"

"Gabrielle said not to grab the chickens by a wing or neck, but instead put our hands gently around their sides."

"How about I keep the crate open, and you catch them."

Deni grinned and nudged her. "Too chicken to catch a chicken?"

"Very funny. And yes." Veronika smiled and bumped her back.

After the little feathered ones were safely captured and locked inside, the girls carried the crate to the man's truck and then followed the sound of Gabrielle's laughter to the kitchen where she and Monsieur Matthias sat at the table drinking tea.

Veronika stayed in the other room where she could

watch and listen. Her eyes stung at the memory of her parents talking and laughing together. So much had been taken from her. Turning around, she wandered outside. A flock of geese passed overhead. If she could fly away, where would she go? Pain held her down like a rock in the pit of her stomach. She could never fly free. She had nothing and no one.

Seventeen

If she couldn't get away in real life, she could at least escape with her painting. Veronika's brush danced watercolors across the canvas as she imagined a salty breeze and sunshine warming her shoulders.

"Lovely." Gabrielle came up from behind her. "Have you been to the ocean?"

"No. I wish I could go."

"This painting is from your imagination?" Surprise registered in her guardian's voice.

"Yes, but I did see paintings like this at a museum."

"I like your turquoise water and bright sand beaches. Your painting reminds me of San Vito Lo Capo in Sicily."

"You have been there?" Veronika turned to survey Gabrielle's face.

"Yes, many, many years ago." Gabrielle smiled with a serene look. "When I was a very little girl."

"Was the ocean beautiful?"

"Yes." Gabrielle stared into the distance for a moment, then her gaze returned to the painting. "Let me show you a technique for your beach scene. The closer to shore, allow the sand to show through the ocean by adding more water to the paint. You can use quick, dry brush strokes to give the impression of foam on the water, adding a touch of fluidity and movement."

Veronika followed her advice, marveling as the painting took on new depth.

"Good. Painting is an escape, an adventure, an opportunity to step into a new scene. Veronika, keep at your craft. God has blessed you with amazing talent. I believe someday your paintings will be in art galleries."

"You think so?" Veronika sat straighter as a feeling of hope rose within her heart.

"Yes." Her mentor smiled and nodded. "Continue working and developing what God has given you."

Fixing her eyes on the painting, Veronika could almost hear the surf, feel the sand under her feet and water covering her ankles. Would the air taste of salt? Would birds float in the sky? Would boats with fishermen be in the distance? A world of possibilities waited for her to explore.

That evening, Veronika rested her head on the back of the couch and half-listened to what was happening around her. She couldn't get over the idea of her paintings someday hanging in a museum or an art gallery. Could something good happen to her? Would it be possible? Maybe if she kept working at her craft, kept learning new techniques, maybe one day she would be able to sell what she painted.

"No one was brave enough to fight the giant Goliath until David arrived to check on his brothers." Gabrielle held open her Bible. "David could not believe the Israelites would let Goliath get away with rudely talking about God and his people. Even though David was only a young boy, he stood in front of King Saul and told him he tended sheep, and when a lion or bear came and took one from his flock, David would fight the mean animals and rescue the sheep. And he knew in the same way, God would help him fight against Goliath."

"Wait, wait." Simone stopped her. "Who sends a boy out to fight lions and bears?" Scowling, Simone crossed her arms. "He did not have good parents."

"Well, back then, that was the culture. I do not believe it was because they were bad parents. David had joined the family business. The sheep needed someone to protect them."

"I still do not like this."

"Even though we might not like to think about a young boy fighting big, mean animals alone, God was with David and used David's time to prepare him for what would happen next in his life. David bravely fought the giant Goliath because the boy knew God would help him win. Surviving difficulties helps us know we *can* survive difficulties."

Veronika sat straighter. "I would rather not go through any bad things."

Deni nodded. "Me neither."

"I think most of us feel that way. But hold on, there's more to the story." Gabrielle continued reading, finishing when David conquered Goliath.

"I love that a little boy beat a giant." Simone jumped to her feet. "I may be little, but maybe I could beat a giant."

Gabrielle chuckled. "I have no doubt, little one. With God's help, nothing is impossible." She then held up a small book with a blank cover and a few pages. "I have a new story for you. Once upon a time, a little girl was raised in a good family, had good food, good parents, and a good life. She went to a good school, got good grades, married a good husband, and died a good old lady. The end." She closed the book. "What do you think?"

"Um, that was boring." Veronika shook her head.

"Why do you think so?"

"There was no adventure."

"Right. Without adventure, danger, and difficulties, the story is boring. In real life, there are those whose stories are harder than others, and the good is often tough to find. However, those who travel in difficult pathways are given the most exciting adventures. Life is a quest, and we are not guaranteed all will go well, but with Jesus Christ in our lives, we are always given a happy ending."

"My momma told me about Jesus." Deni's voice was quiet, reverent.

Gabrielle gazed her way. "Do you remember?"

"A little. When you pray, you say he is God's son?"

"Yes, Jesus Christ is God's son who came to the world, lived a sinless life, and willingly sacrificed himself for our sins—the bad things we have done. He was crucified on a cross, died, and then rose again. And if we believe in him, he will forgive and give us eternal life with him in heaven where there is no pain or crying, no bad people, and nothing evil."

Tears pooled in Deni's eyes. "I want that."

Gabrielle took her hand in hers. "Would you be willing to pray and ask Jesus to be the Lord of your life and come to live in your heart?" At Deni's teary nod, their mentor said, "Dear Heavenly Father, thank you for your son, Jesus Christ."

Deni followed along as Gabrielle continued. "I ask

you would forgive me for my sins, for the wrong things I have done. I believe Jesus died for my sins and was raised to life. I give my heart to Jesus Christ as my Savior. And I want to follow Him as Lord from this day forward. Guide and help me to do your will. I pray this in the name of Jesus Christ, who is my Savior. Amen."

With tears streaming down her cheeks, Deni sighed. "I feel so light and free."

"I am proud of you." Gabrielle hugged her tight. "Welcome to the family of God."

Veronika stared at the floor. How could she trust a God who let her suffer? Why would she trust and give her heart to someone who allowed people to be abused and beaten? No, this was not for her.

Rising to her feet, she stepped past the others, and climbed the stairs to bed. She would take care of herself. She could not trust Gabrielle's God.

The next day, after chores and schoolwork were done, Veronika held her sketch pad and wandered through the field. A slight movement under a purple flower drew her attention. Leaning down, she smiled at a tiny rabbit hunched in the grass. With soft, careful motions, she settled near her furry friend and flipped open her sketch pad.

A memory of the story of Peter Rabbit made her smile. "Hello, little Peter. Are you out exploring?" Veronika sketched the little rabbit as a story formulated of Peter going on his first solo outing. She held up the pad. "Do you like?" His little nose twitched. "I will take that as a yes. Now, what would you wear?"

At the sound of approaching footsteps, she held up her hand before Deni and the dog came closer. "Shh, be quiet. Please do not scare my friend."

Tiptoeing close, Deni's smile signaled she understood as she settled nearby in the grass with Woof by her side.

Veronika continued to sketch, at times showing Deni what she'd completed.

Deni picked at the grass and let out a loud sigh.

"What?" Veronika's pencil kept moving across the paper.

"Last night, you walked away and did not seem happy when I prayed to Jesus. I have never felt such peace. Why are you not happy for me?"

Deni's voice stopped her pencil mid-sketch. "That is your decision."

"Christ could also be yours."

Veronika closed her pad and glared at her friend. "If God is a saving God. If Jesus Christ is a savior, why did they not save us?"

"We were saved. It could have been worse. We could have been killed."

Veronika slapped her pencil down on her sketch pad. "Death would have been better than living with death inside. I am breathing, but part of me has died. My family was taken, my life was taken, and my soul was taken. What was lost *will* not and can*not* be replaced."

"But Jesus makes all things new. Gabrielle says all things work together for good to those who love God."

"Stop." Veronika held up her hand. "I wanted a quiet moment without someone lecturing or telling me things I don't believe. I am glad you have found peace, Deni. I want the best for you. I want you to be happy.

But now you must accept me as I am."

Deni looked down, then glanced at her with kind but sad eyes. "Veronika, you will always be my friend, and I will always be here for you. And, whether you like it or not, I will pray you find the peace of Christ in your own heart." Deni rose to her feet and walked away.

The rabbit raced into the trees.

Clutching her sketch pad, Veronika jumped up and stared at the back of her retreating friend. Why did everyone have to pressure her? Why couldn't they leave her alone? She had listened to Gabrielle's constant stories about Jesus, about people forgiving and moving on with their lives, brokenness being fixed, blah, blah, blah, lecture, lecture, lecture.

Veronika kicked at the thick grass as she stomped to the trees, followed by the dog. Shaking her head, she passed the tree that had been hit by lightning. The stupid tree did not choose to keep living; it just happened. Some things healed and some did not.

She was sick of the country, sick of chickens that pecked her fingers, sick of bossy cows and woofy dogs. Why couldn't she move to a big city, live in an apartment, and find a job where she could work and buy the things she wanted? Maybe the next time Isabella or Mikhail came for a visit, she could go to the city with them, and they would help her find a job.

Veronika walked deeper into the trees. Her schoolwork was going well, and she could speak several languages, but what would be available for work? Maybe a secretary or factory worker. Then again, she would need a better job, something to support her and Deni.

A bird twilled a haunting tune in a spindly tree above her head. Veronika turned and ran headfirst into a spider web. Flailing and screaming, she frantically wiped at her face, her hair, her clothes, and ran forward as branches scraped at her arms. Ahead the pathway lightened as the trees thinned. She hurried toward the light, then at the sound of men's voices she stopped. Woof leaned against her legs and let out a low growl. Skin pebbling with goose bumps, she hid behind a tree. Two older men talked as they worked the vines of the vineyard.

"Hello, pretty." A deep voice behind her caused her to quake.

Fear trickling down her spine, she whirled and faced a tanned man with dark hair and brown eyes.

Still growling, Woof stood in front of her.

The man raised his hands as he glanced at the dog and then at her. "I meant no harm, but you are on my property."

"Your property?" She held her sketchpad against her chest and staggered back.

"Yes, welcome to Chateau Marcella vineyard." He smiled. "My name is Henri. Would you like a tour?"

"No, thank you. I must not." She shook her head.

He surveyed her for a moment. "You are living with Gabrielle?"

"Yes." Hoping her beating heart couldn't be seen through her shirt, heat crept up her face.

"She is a nice lady." His lips coiled into a smile.

She swallowed, nodded.

"I would have thought perhaps you were a model looking for a place for a photo shoot."

Vision tunneling, her breath ragged against her dry throat, she bent over.

"Are you okay?"

Woof's growl intensified as he blocked the man from coming closer.

She touched the big dog to steady herself. Dragged in air as the dizziness passed. Straightening her back, she lifted her chin but did not speak.

"I meant no harm." His dark eyes surveyed her as his gaze traveled her body.

Veronika took another step back, grateful the big dog kept his body against her legs.

"You are beautiful. Please forgive me. I did not mean that as an insult. Someone like you could make a fortune at modeling."

Without a reply, she grabbed the big dog and whispered in his ear. "Show me the way home."

Running away, she did not stop until she was safe inside the house.

Eighteen

The ringing phone drew Veronika from her nightmarish sleep. The man had told her she was beautiful, but the look in his eyes still made her skin crawl. She never should have wandered so close to that property. Would she ever feel safe? She wiped her eyes, then put on her robe and padded down the hallway, stopping at the doorway to Gabrielle's room.

Standing by her bedside, with her back turned away, Gabrielle held the phone to her ear. "Yes, we will be careful." A pause. "I understand." Shoulders sagging, she hung up the phone. She straightened and gazed at the ceiling. "God help us."

Veronika stepped inside the room. "Is everything okay?"

Whirling around, Gabrielle stared at her. For a moment, she said nothing, then pointed to the chairs by her window. "Come, sit with me."

Pulse pounding in her ears, Veronika sat and waited.

Gabrielle took a deep breath and blew it out slowly. "What I'm about to tell you will be shocking." Her voice was kind but strained. She took Veronika's cold hands in hers. "What happened to your family was not an accident."

"*What?*" Veronika doubled over as flashes of the

terrible wreck ran through her mind.

"I am so sorry." Gabrielle squeezed her hands, held them gently but tight. "Your family was murdered, and you were not supposed to survive. Your uncle is a very prominent man in your country's government, and evil people tried to force him to do what they wanted. Veronika, your uncle did not know you were alive. He is why you were rescued from Tatiana's and brought here for safety."

"Why did you not tell me?" Tears stung her eyes and angry heat boiled inside. "Why has my uncle not come for me?"

"Your uncle loves you very much, but he knows if anyone saw you with him, the bad people would not stop. Most of them have been caught, but someone is still ...."

Nika recoiled. "After me?"

"Yes. The police thought they had gotten everyone, but your uncle just received another letter. That's one of the reasons I've asked you to be careful when you are outside."

Heat slithered up Veronika's spine. She should never have talked to Henri.

"Don't worry, Isabella is coming to stay with us for a few days." Gabrielle smothered her in a hug.

Veronika remained in the embrace but kept her body stiff. They should have told her about her uncle. They should have told her about her family. All this time, she thought she had been abandoned. Then again, hadn't she been left on her own? If her uncle was that prominent, why didn't he use his position to come and get her? Why was she left to rot? Veronika pulled away and stared at the floor.

"Do you want to talk?" Gabrielle lifted her chin and gazed into her eyes. "It's going to be okay. I'm here for you."

Veronika nodded, then walked back to her room and crawled into bed. What was okay? It had been years since anything was all right. She was tired of her life, tired of trying to survive. It was time to take things into her own hands. If someone was out to get her, let them try. She would be ready to fight.

* * *

For two weeks, Isabella had shadowed her every move. Leaning back, Veronika studied her latest painting. Swishing her brush in the water, she wiped it dry with a cloth. Perhaps a darker color would give the shading she needed. After dabbing her brush in the paint, she made careful strokes and finally achieved the look she desired.

"You are very talented." Isabella stood next to her.

Even though the compliment was nice, Veronika tried not to growl. She couldn't get away or have a moment to herself.

"Momma G. also showed me how to paint." Isabella sat next to her. "She told me that even if we mess up, the canvas doesn't change. In the same way, although we can't alter our past, our timeless God takes the mess thrown across our life's canvas and creates a new creation, his masterpiece."

Veronika didn't comment, she just kept painting.

"Did you know the name Nika means bringing

victory, and Veronika means truth," Isabella said. "The plaque in the other room reads *Veritas Vos Liberabit*, which means the truth will set you free. Jesus Christ is the life, the way, and the truth. He loves you and wants to set you free and show you the way to a new life."

Veronika rolled her eyes. She would like just one day without someone trying to ram religion down her throat. The truth was the only way she would make it through this life was by her own strength.

"Perhaps someday you will be an artist and have an art gallery. Never give up on your dreams, Veronika. Anything is possible with God." Isabella patted her shoulder and left the room.

Huffing, Veronika shook her head and rammed her brush in the water. God made things possible for other people. Not her. She had lost her family—lost more than anyone would ever know—and now someone was still after her. If her future held possibilities, it was because she would do them on her own. She would be brave and strong and find a way to survive.

Henri's comments came to mind. Could she be a model? How could she stand in front of a camera after what had been done to her? Then again, that was Nika, not who she was now. She was Veronika, and Veronika could do as she pleased. Even Gabrielle had said all things work together for good. Veronika smiled. If she could make a fortune, as Henri had said, she could take the bad and work it in her favor. Perhaps her looks would be the truth that brought victory.

That night, Veronika lay in bed thinking of the ways she could start a new life. Painting was a possibility, but modeling or acting could offer a bigger opportunity.

She would start working on her posture, how she walked, and work with her hair to develop new hairstyles.

The stairway creaked, and she stilled. She glanced at Deni, her breathing measured and quiet. Another noise came from downstairs. Veronika grabbed her robe and tiptoed down the hall. Gabrielle's unmade bed was empty.

Taking a calming breath, Veronika waited and listened. Glass shattered downstairs. The sound of the front door opening and closing echoed from below.

Staying quiet, she moved in the shadows, avoiding the stair that creaked. The room below was dark, with no sign of Isabella. Even the porch light was off.

Where was everyone? If something had happened, wouldn't Woof have barked? Should she creep back upstairs and wait for them to come back inside? Instead, she edged to the window and peeked outside. A light flickered in the barn, then went out.

Was something wrong? Should she wake Deni and check on Simone? Hurrying back upstairs, she breathed a sigh of relief to find both girls still asleep. Taking a deep breath, Veronika returned downstairs and tried to decide what she should do.

In the darkness, a figure moved toward her. "Nika, how are you?" A female voice from her past whispered.

Chills skidded up Veronika's arms as Andrea, the lady who worked in the orphanage kitchen, came into view.

Dressed in a black turtleneck and black slacks, Andrea moved catlike toward her. "I came to check on you." Her voice remained quiet.

Veronika stepped back. "Where are Gabrielle and Isabella?"

"They are in the barn waiting for you." Andrea's voice held a syrupy sweetness that made Veronika's skin crawl with tiny spiders. "Follow me. I will take you to them."

Though the night's warmth blanketed her, Veronika shivered as they walked forward. The half-moon cast eerie shadows, and in the distance, an animal howled.

Shoved through the barn door, Veronika dug in her heels. Gabrielle and Isabella were gagged and tied on the floor. The big dog lay motionless at their feet.

Veronika whirled around and stared at a knife blade glinting in the moonlight.

"You have gotten away one too many times," Andrea growled through gritted teeth. She slapped Nika's face hard. "Get on your knees."

Holding her stinging cheek, Veronika dropped to her knees in the dirt and hay.

The woman walked to a canvas bag and pulled out a camera. "One more picture for your dear uncle."

The flash momentarily blinded Veronika.

"This time, if he doesn't pay, he will be next. I am tired of you all."

Shuddering, Veronika stared at the woman. "Why do you do this?"

"*Why?*" Her voice rose an octave. "Such a stupid question." She spit the words. "Where there is power, there is a need for control, and your uncle needed controlling." She jabbed the knife toward Isabella.

"People like *you* neutralized my team. Of course, Tatiana tried to use the situation for her advantage. You probably did me a favor with her. Plus, Isabella, it was you who led me here."

Andrea then pivoted to Veronika. "Now, I'm cleaning up this mess so I can frame your uncle and move on to my next project." She placed the camera back in the bag and removed a cigarette lighter. "I'm sorry to say, there will be a terrible fire. The house and barn will burn to the ground. Such a shame so many lives will be lost."

Veronika fisted her hands. She could not, *would* not, let her friends be killed. Propelling herself forward from her knees, she vaulted into Andrea's chest and plowed her to the ground. Screaming, she threw wild punches at the woman's face.

As blood spurted from Andrea's nose, she cried out in fury, rolled Veronika off her, and sprang to her feet.

Andrea pointed the knife at her. "You will pay for this, you little brat." The evil woman's gaze murderous, she stood over Veronika and kicked her over and over and over.

A gunshot split the air.

Andrea's eyes went wide as a red stain grew on her chest. Stumbling forward, she collapsed.

Mikhail stepped out of the shadows, his gun drawn.

Nineteen
1972 – Paris, France

Coffee cup in hand, Veronika stepped out on the balcony of her apartment and admired the red blooming flowers in terracotta pots. Early morning sunshine streamed across the floor as new life burst forth in spring colors across the city of Paris. Her uncle's passing and the money he'd left her had given her the opportunity for a new life. Much to Gabrielle's dislike, Veronika had moved to Paris and taken Deni with her.

"Good morning!" Deni's cheerful voice came from the kitchen. "Today at eight, we must be at the Eiffel Tower for your next photo shoot."

"I will be ready." The last few years had been a whirlwind as her career skyrocketed. Her acting and modeling career, with her friend as her agent and business partner, allowed her to live as she wanted. Every time she stood in front of a camera, she stood tall thinking of how she had made something good out of the evil in her past. No longer did people use her. She used her beauty for her own purposes, and as a result her bank account and fame continued to grow.

"Happy anniversary." Deni handed her a tarte aux fruits. "I made it with fresh strawberries."

"Anniversary?"

"This is the seventh year since we were rescued."

"Ah, so it is. Thank you, dear friend." Thankfully, those horrid years seemed long ago. She had survived the orphanage, Tatiana, and Andrea's assassination attempt. And now she had the world at her feet.

"I meant to tell you Momma G. called last night while you were out. She didn't say anything, but I think she is still a little hurt that you did not join us for Isabella and Mikhail's wedding last week. She always asks about you."

"How is she?" Even though she appreciated what Gabrielle had done for them, she'd not remained close to the woman.

"She is well," Deni continued. "She has two new girls who came last week. Momma G. was pleased you were continuing to paint."

Savoring the strawberry bliss made by her friend, Veronika smiled. "The ones I took to the gallery have sold, and the rest are receiving positive feedback." Her career paid the bills, but art gave her a place to put her heart.

"Oh, and on other news, Simone eloped with Monsieur Matthias's grandson and is doing well."

Veronika lifted an eyebrow. "I am not surprised. The year before we left, he was always finding an excuse to help around the farm." Although the boy was nice, Simone should have joined them in the city instead of wasting her life in the country.

"Love is in the air." Deni gave her an impish grin. "So, how are things going with Charles?"

"Six months today." Heat flushed Veronika's neck at the mention of the handsome, debonair, six-foot-three movie star who had swept her off her feet during an acting assignment she had in his movie.

"I can't believe you're dating a film star. But since you are one of France's top models, as well as an actress, it should be no surprise to us."

"All because of my wonderful agent." Veronika grinned.

"Ha. You would do fine without me, but I am grateful to help."

"And how are you and Jean-Paul?"

"Very well, *merci*. He is such a kind man."

"Are you sure you want to keep dating him?" Although Jean-Paul was a likable man, he was a widower, ten years older than Deni, with two children.

"His little boys are very sweet. I hate that they lost their mother at such young ages. I have never known anyone like Jean-Paul." Deni's eyes took on a dreamy look. "He is a gentleman, and he loves Jesus."

Taking a bite of food, Veronika avoided commenting. Deni's faith was not one they shared.

A knock on the door sent Veronika scurrying to answer. "That must be Charles."

As soon as she opened the door, he wrapped her in his arms and nuzzled her neck. "Veronika, my fabulous supermodel. You always smell so nice."

She kissed him long and deep, then led him down the hall. "Deni, look who is here."

"Hello, Charles. How are you today?"

"Great." He didn't seem to notice Deni's lack of enthusiasm at his presence. "This afternoon, we wrap up shooting, and I will be free for a month before my next film."

"Congratulations."

"Thank you. And..." He turned toward Veronika. "If my fabulous V. can get away, I would love to take you to check out a villa I may buy in the south of France and see what you think."

Veronika's heart jumped at the thought. She grinned and turned to Deni. "Perhaps my agent will let me take a little vacation time?"

A cloud crossed her friend's face before she nodded. "You are free for a few days, but do not forget your photo shoot coming up in Japan."

"I will be ready. You worry too much."

Charles took Veronika in his arms and twirled her around. "Call me when you finish. Pack your bags. I promise to show you an amazing time." He waggled his eyebrows, then gave her a kiss worthy of a steamy, romantic movie.

After he left, Deni turned toward her. "You are going away with him? Do you know where you will stay?"

"Do not be such a prude. He loves me. Everything will be fine."

"I worry about you."

"Stop. You were upset when I dated many men, and now you are mad because I am dating one man."

"I wish you could find someone who loves God. I want the best for you. You know I'll keep praying for you."

"We have been over this before." Veronika walked away, then turned back. "You have what works for you. I will make my own way."

Exhausted and jet-lagged, Veronika shuffled out of her bedroom, down the hall of her apartment, and gazed out the window at the lights of Paris. Jerked wide awake by a weird nightmare, sleep had eluded her. Maybe she could curl up on the couch and watch the sunrise.

A light flipped on in the kitchen.

Deni, still in her pajamas, peeked around the corner. "What are you doing up?"

"I could not sleep."

"Me neither." Bible in hand, Deni plopped next to her. "I thought I needed to spend time reading. I've had awful dreams since you got back."

"Gee, thanks."

"No, it's not you. I think it's those things." She pointed to the coffee table and the little statues Veronika had brought back from Asia. "Would you mind getting rid of them?"

"Why? They are mementos from my trip."

"No, they represent something evil. They are idols of foreign gods."

Veronika scoffed. "Seriously? You worry too much." She gathered them up. "But for you, I will put them in my room, so you do not have to worry."

"Merci. But perhaps it would be best if you threw them away. You have other things from your trip."

"I will think about it." She didn't believe in Deni's religious stuff, but for her best friend's sake, Veronika carried them to her room and placed them on her dresser. Leaning closer, she studied the little statues. Goosebumps rose on her arms. They did seem a touch disturbing.

Veronika lay on her bed and turned away from the statues. Next week, she would go away again with Charles to the villa. They could swim in his pool or the ocean, dine at the café in the little town nearby, and walk along the beach.

She drifted off to sleep, imagining spending time with her lover.

Bathed in sweat, she again jolted from a nightmare and turned over to stare at the little statues. Without hesitating, she jumped to her feet, threw them in the trash, and placed the bag outside her apartment door before returning to bed. Almost immediately, she fell into a peaceful sleep.

"Good morning, sleepyhead." Deni's cheerful voice woke her. "Time to get up. You have an assignment in two hours."

Veronika opened and closed one eye. How her friend could be so cheerful this early in the morning, she could not comprehend. She yawned. "I'll be up soon."

Deni jostled her shoulder. "It will take thirty minutes to drive there. You need to get up now. I have pastries and coffee waiting in the kitchen."

Groaning, Veronika threw back her covers. She'd not had another nightmare, but she was exhausted. Traveling internationally had kicked her tail. After her shower, she dressed and yawned her way to the kitchen.

"You will not believe this." Deni shoved a newspaper into her hands and pointed to an article. "A man found an old oil painting in a trash bin. When he got home, he intended to paint over the old canvas. So, he carefully removed the upper layers of grime, dirt, and a poorly painted landscape, only to discover a masterpiece that had been missing for over a century. Wouldn't it be fun to find something like that?"

"Yes. I will keep my eyes open for any old canvases now." Veronika chuckled. "But I will not spend my life rooting through trash bins." She took a sip of her coffee from the delicate China cup.

"I won't either, but wouldn't Momma G. love this story? She'd tell us that no matter what happened in our life, the master painter knows the masterpiece under the canvas."

Veronika sipped her coffee and shook her head. No matter where she went, the God stories followed her. If she didn't love Deni like a sister, she would end their friendship. She had made her own life without God's help, and she would continue. She was known as the Fabulous V., and the press fawned all over her. Magazines wanted her on their covers, and Charles loved her.

She'd taken her grimy life and made a masterpiece because of what she had done, not God. And nothing would stand in the way of her success.

Twenty

Deni's stepsons ran and played in the enclosed yard where she lived with her husband, Jean-Paul. Since she'd married, Deni had stepped with ease into the role of stepmother.

"Are you happy still?" Veronika watched the boys tumble in the grass.

"Wonderfully happy." Deni's face seemed to glow as she rubbed her growing belly. "Our first anniversary is next week."

The boys tussled in the flowerbed, kicking up dirt. How Deni ever kept them clean was a mystery.

"No regrets?"

"None." Deni grinned widely. "You should try marriage, Nika. Do you and Charles have any plans?"

"No. We do not discuss marriage." Their relationship had focused on fun and excitement as they traveled and enjoyed the limelight of the press. They lived in the moment. Deep conversations were unnecessary. She avoided speaking of the past, and her dreams of a future together remained unspoken, except for that one night. The night they had drunk their fill of expensive champagne and her deepest secrets were revealed. Charles listened, consoled, and pledged never to speak of what she had gone through in the past. Her past was a mess but what now would become of her future?

Veronika waited until the boys were at the far end of the yard and turned to her friend. "I am pregnant."

"You're what?" Deni's mouth gaped open. "What are you going to do? Is Charles going to marry you? Does he know?"

"I have not told him. He is still in Italy working on his movie."

"Oh, Veronika. You will keep the baby, right? You know I will be here for you."

"How can I model or go on an acting job with a bulging belly?"

"You can figure out something. Charles loves you; he will be happy."

"I am not so sure." How could she possibly mother a child? Someone like her didn't deserve to be a mother.

A cry came from one of Deni's sons. The five-year-old ran to Deni, tears running down his dirty cheeks, and pointed to a tiny cut on his finger. She kissed his hand, and his tears dried. He ran back to play.

"I thought you had a good relationship with Charles," Deni said.

"Since he has been in Italy, his calls have been infrequent. Have you seen the actress in his movie? She is beautiful."

Deni's soft gaze rested on her. "Veronika, no one is as beautiful as you."

"You are my friend, and you are kind. The last time Charles flew home, he was distracted and said he had much on his mind. I saw photos in the newspapers of him with his leading lady at a restaurant. He did not seem distracted with her."

"He probably was on a publicity shoot. You know how those things work. When will he finish his movie?"

"Next month." Veronika paused before she voiced the fear that had grown with her pregnancy. "What if he does not come back?"

"He will return." Deni spoke soothing words. The villa is his home. He doesn't look at any woman like he looks at you. He wants you, and I believe he would want your baby."

"I am not mother material. You know that. I am not like you."

"You would make a great mother."

"No," Veronika scoffed. "But if I did have this baby, I would not send it away. I would never let my child be treated as we were."

"You will not let that happen." Deni reached for her hand. "Please promise me you will talk to Charles before you do anything rash. If you do not, I will call him."

"Do *not* call him, or our friendship is over." Veronika spat the words and pulled away her hand.

"Why would you say that?"

Veronika rose to her feet. "This is my decision."

"Yes, that's true, but your decision will affect others, and more importantly, whatever you decide will affect you."

"I do not know what I will do. For now, I need your help. Book modeling jobs for me wearing coats and jackets. Call the photographer and set up sessions around the city and countryside. I need photos we can share over the next few months. Whatever I decide, I do not want anyone to know."

Deni's eyes shimmered as she stood next to her. "I understand. I will pray for you. Just this once, would you pray too? And please don't be mad at me. I promise not to call Charles, but you should. It is his decision too."

Veronika spent the next two hours walking the streets of Paris. Everywhere she turned, there were mothers pushing strollers, children skipping and playing on the sidewalks, and even the clothing shops advertised for children.

A group of girls squealed and ran to her. "V! Can we have your autograph?" Thrusting papers and a pen in her hands, they gathered around her.

Veronika smiled, signed her name, and posed for photographs. Once finished, they ran off and left her standing alone.

How would she survive, and where would she go if not for her career? Even though her uncle had left her a substantial amount of money, she was now an orphan. If she had a child, no one would help her. Deni said she would, but she was busy with her own children. Veronika thought a moment. Maybe Deni would be willing to raise the baby. Then again, her husband probably would not want to raise another man's child.

Deni asked her to pray. What use was there in praying? She got herself in this mess, and one way or another, she would get herself out of it.

Keeping her head down, Veronika continued walking. The scent of baked goods wafted from an outside café, causing her stomach to churn. She had worked hard for her career and made a name for herself. Her modeling and acting hinged on a slender figure.

Veronika laid her hand on her belly. Even though no one could tell, a life grew inside. A deep, howling ache welled up within her at the unfairness of life. She dropped her hand.

Deni was happy in her marriage and with being a mom. Why couldn't she be happy? *Because broken things birth broken things.*

Back at her apartment, Veronika slouched on the couch and stared out the window at the sunset. Charles constantly traveled for his movies. If she kept the baby, what guarantees would she have that he wouldn't leave her? She'd be stuck alone with a child. If she took care of things and Charles found out later, would he hate her? Then again, would he hate her if she kept the baby?

Rising to her feet, she shuffled into Deni's old room. She had turned it into her art studio and now immersed herself in a painting of a ship on a stormy sea. Hours passed.

Her alarm chimed at midnight, signaling it was time. Charles had a right to know. Veronika dialed the number of the hotel room where he was staying during filming.

He picked up on the third ring. His voice, although pleasant, held a terse tone.

She cringed as she told him the news.

Charles paused. "Are you sure?"

"Yes."

"I didn't expect this. Let me think. I must finish filming here. Wait, are you thinking of, you know, keeping it?"

Veronika stared out her dark window and couldn't reply. Her voice would betray her.

He blew out a breath. "Fine. You can stay at the villa for now."

"For now?"

"That didn't come out right." He almost growled. "I've got lots on my plate right now. I can't think."

Noises and movement could be heard in the background of his call.

A female voice giggled. "Charles, you're wanted on the set."

"Veronika, I must go. I'll call you tomorrow, okay? I need time to process."

She hung up without saying another word. She had his answer.

Twenty-One

The amber liquid in her glass tempted her, promising to wash away her worries and help her forget her troubles. Blowing out a breath, Veronika threw the spirits in the sink and turned away. She couldn't drink. Not now. Why had she gotten pregnant? She had taken precautions. Her life finally had been on a positive trajectory. Her career had risen to the top. Her bank account expanded with monthly payments for her work. Now, everything would change. If anyone found out about her pregnancy, the photographers would stop calling, company sponsors would vanish, and even her acting jobs would disappear. No one wanted a pregnant model or actress.

Curling up on her couch, she stared out her apartment window. The city wakened to a new day. Delivery trucks rumbled in the street below, the café on the corner would set up for their new day, and tourists would wander the streets. Life would go on while hers had stopped. She was sure another woman had been in the background when she talked to Charles on the phone. Probably his beautiful co-star. He said nothing was going on between them, but the photos in the paper clearly showed lust or love in their eyes as they looked at one another.

A knock on her door sounded. She didn't want to

talk to anyone or see anyone. The knock persisted. Groaning, she walked down the hall and peered through the peephole. Charles stood outside holding red roses.

Veronika sucked in a breath and let him inside.

He wrapped his arms around her and held her close. "Oh, babe. I'm sorry about when you called. I was distracted."

She leaned against his chest, his heart beating strong in her ear.

He stepped back and handed her the roses. "Forgive me?"

She took the flowers from him and went to the kitchen to find a vase.

He came up behind her and again wrapped her in his arms. "Move into the villa. Have the baby there."

"You did not sound happy the other night." After filling the vase, she arranged the flowers.

"I'm sorry. The news was unexpected. One minute, things are heading in one direction, then life throws a curveball."

Veronika turned toward him and pushed him away. "I did not do this on purpose."

"Right. We'll take care of things. Come away with me to the villa. My staff is loyal and sworn to secrecy."

"I still have a few jobs to complete this month."

He trailed behind her as she moved to the den. "Okay, come when you're finished."

"People will not be pleased we are having a child and not married." Veronika sat on the couch, surveying him.

"It's the seventies. Let them think what they want.

People are such prudes. We can keep it quiet. The villa is private and remote." He sat on the couch and propped his feet on her coffee table. "No one needs to know if you don't want them to. Once the baby comes, we can hire a nanny and get on with our lives. Trust me."

Veronika swallowed hard. Could she believe him, and could she really trust him?

* * *

"Thank you for these." Veronika surveyed the maternity clothes laid across her bed. Maybe if all went well, she and Charles could make it work, and maybe she could be a good mother to her child.

Deni smiled. "The pants might be a little short since you're taller, but I know you can make them work. You always look good no matter what you wear."

"Thank you, friend." Veronika folded and packed the clothes in the open suitcase. "I leave in the morning for the villa. I will miss you."

"I'll miss you too. But I'll come see you. Jean-Paul said he would keep the children so I could be there for the baby's birth."

"I appreciate that. It has been hard keeping all this a secret. No one has noticed anything. Except for the photographer yesterday who said my chest was expanding. He did not seem to mind that fact."

"I'm sure he didn't. It's been easy to hide the pregnancy with the winter weather to keep you in coats for your assignments." Deni helped her fold a shirt. "Have you talked anymore about marriage to Charles?"

Trying to release the growing tension, Veronika rolled her shoulders. "No. He does not mention such things."

Deni stopped and surveyed her. "Have you asked him?"

"No."

"He got you pregnant. I don't think it's an imposition to ask him to marry you."

"Stop." Veronika slammed shut her suitcase. "I do not want to talk about this again." She couldn't explain why Charles had not asked her to marry him and why they continued their lives as though nothing had happened. Hurt burned in her chest. She was good enough to share his bed but not his name.

"I'm sorry." Deni hugged her. "I want the best for you. I'll keep praying for you."

"Thank you. Maybe your God will hear."

Twenty-Two

Bundling her coat around her and her swollen belly, Veronika stepped out on the villa balcony and stared at the sea. The home she shared with Charles was lovely, and the view was breathtaking. The house staff cared for her every need and fed her well, but none were particularly friendly. She spent most of her days reading or walking along the beach. Yet, even with the beauty and comforts of her self-imposed exile, her doubts about her relationship with Charles continued to grow. The pregnancy continued to be a secret to the outside world, but the rumors in the papers said she had a breakdown. Charles did nothing to stop that rumor.

Even though he was somewhat attentive to her, his phone calls were rare when he traveled. His excuse was that his movie directors demanded his time, his days were long, and his nights were spent rehearsing his lines. She understood that process, but she also knew there would be time to call if he really wanted. Plus, several times when he was at the villa, she'd caught him whispering on the phone. When she walked into the room, he would quickly hang up.

The baby kicked, and she rubbed her hand across her belly. "You will be here soon, little one. Perhaps things will change when you arrive." The midwife had told her it would be another week. Veronika sighed.

The waiting made time crawl at an uncomfortable snail's pace.

How she wished she could have been there for Deni during the birth of her baby girl, but Charles convinced Veronika she shouldn't travel during her pregnancy. Even though Deni's new baby girl was only six months old, she was scheduled to arrive in a few days. Thankfully, Jean-Paul had graciously agreed to keep the children to allow Deni to come to stay with her at the villa. If only Charles was as gracious.

* * *

"It's a boy." The midwife smiled at Charles as she held up the tiny screaming baby.

"Please, may I hold him?" Veronika held out her hands.

The midwife ignored her and took the baby to clean, measure, and weigh him. Once she was finished, she wrapped him in a blanket and handed him to Charles.

He smiled and cradled the baby against his chest. "Welcome to the world, James Olivier Fontaine."

Veronika struggled to sit and reached for the baby. "Please, may I see him?"

With a flat expression, Charles surveyed her a moment, then handed the baby to her.

She held the tiny bundle against her breast. Tiny blue eyes gazed at her, and his hand wrapped around her finger. She'd never felt such love. Sobbing, she held him tight. He was hers to love and hold.

"Thank you for your services." Charles addressed

the midwife. "You realize you are to never talk to anyone about this?" He handed the woman a large sum of cash.

Smiling, the lady nodded and took the money. "I won't say a word. Enjoy your son, Mr. Fontaine."

"I will. Thank you." He continued quietly talking to the woman as he walked her to the door and down the hallway.

Veronika held her baby, amazed at how right this felt. The delivery had been horribly painful but so worth it. How amazing that a tiny, healthy, little body came from her. How could something so perfect come from something as broken as her? She kissed his blond downy head. "Welcome to the world, sweet James."

Charles returned with a glass of water. After setting it on the table next to her, he took the baby from her arms. "James is perfect. He weighed in at six pounds twelve ounces. Not bad for coming early." He rested his hand on the little one's back and beamed with pride. "Take a drink. I'm sure you are famished."

Veronika gulped the fluid and recoiled. "This does not taste good." She handed him back the glass.

He pushed it back toward her. "Your taste buds probably aren't working right after the birth." He smiled. "Drink it all. You need your strength."

She complied as he stood by the bed watching her.

His eyes shimmering, he cuddled the baby. "You will be happy here. I'll make sure you are always happy."

"*We* will make sure."

Charles nodded. "I have hired a nanny to ensure you have someone to help."

Veronika smiled. "I think I can manage. And Deni will be here in a few days."

"Deni won't be able to stay long, and I want to ensure my son has the best care."

She tilted her head. "*Our* son will have the best care."

"Yes, I'll make sure of that."

Nausea rolled in her stomach, and her vision blurred. "I am not feeling well."

"I'm sure that's natural after giving birth." Charles leaned close, surveying her face. "Rest. Your body has been through a major event. I need to make a few phone calls. I'll be back later to check on you." With James in his arms, he left the room.

The room was spinning, and Veronika gripped the covers. She wished Deni was here so she could ask if this reaction was normal. Did everyone feel this bad after giving birth? Curling into a ball, she tried not to be sick in her bed.

The next few days passed in a blur as she stayed so sick she could barely get out of bed to visit the bathroom. When she was at her sickest, Charles and the midwife came asking Veronika to sign the paperwork for the baby. The staff brought food, mainly soup, to her room for meals. Charles never came to see her again, and no one would bring her the baby.

* * *

"He's perfect." Smiling, Deni sat in the chair next to her in the nursery.

"Yes." Relieved to finally feel better and have James

in her arms, Veronika nestled the baby against her chest. "Deni, I am worried. Charles does not seem himself. He is thrilled about the baby but rarely looks at me."

"I'm sure everything is fine. He's probably just a proud poppa. Is the baby nursing well?"

"No. Charles put James on a bottle. He said I was too sick to nurse."

"I'm sorry you were so sick."

"I really felt awful. Did you feel terrible after you gave birth?"

Deni shrugged, her smile gentle. "Well, I didn't feel great. It's a big change. Even after six months, I'm still trying to get rid of the extra weight I put on with my pregnancy. You must have lost every additional pound right after James's birth."

"I was so sick I weigh less than when I got pregnant."

"I'm so sorry you were that ill."

Veronika kissed the downy soft top of James's head. "Charles questions me about everything. He says I am not changing the baby the right way or bathing the baby the right way. He even said I am not feeding the baby the right way."

"Well, maybe he is just overprotective since it's his first child."

"*Our* first child."

Deni wore a puzzled expression. "Yes, both of you are the parents."

"Charles has hired a nanny."

"A nanny? I guess it would be nice to have an extra set of hands."

"She is not very nice. The staff here treats me nice, but I know they are loyal to Charles."

"Well, you are the employer. You tell the nanny what to do and not to do, and you decide how much time you want her to help."

"I guess so." Trying to tell that woman anything had been difficult. Veronika nestled James tighter against her chest.

"I haven't seen anything about the baby in the press. I'm surprised Charles didn't announce James to the world."

"With our careers, he thought it best not to say anything. Charles took time off from his movie, telling them he had a personal problem. He didn't mention to the press that he had a child."

"Is he not going to marry you?"

"Things are not good between us. Deni, please pray for me, for us, for James?"

"I always pray for you, my friend. And I will pray for your family. You know, you could also pray."

"I have." Her prayers for her parents and brother did not save them from death. What good would it do to pray now? But for her son, she would always pray. How could God not listen to prayers for someone so innocent?

"You can always count on my prayers. God loves you, Veronika. And God loves your baby. I'm sorry I can't be here all the time with you. But you know you can always call me."

"Thank you. Pray, though, okay? Pray for James and me."

Her expression troubled, Deni laid her hand on

Veronika's arm. "I will. Is there something else that is bothering you?"

"I am not sure. Maybe I just worry."

Deni knelt next to Veronika's chair and prayed for her friend.

Twenty-Three

Mrs. Badeau, the older woman Charles hired as a nanny, was a nightmare. Since her arrival the woman had questioned Veronika about everything she did with James, making her feel less than adequate with her own child and barely giving her time with the baby.

Grateful for a moment alone, Veronika sang a lullaby as she cradled and rocked James in her arms. He cooed, and she would swear he smiled at her.

The nursery door banged open, and Mrs. Badeau crossed the tile floor and stood over her. "*Miss* Zabelle, I would advise you to stop coddling the baby. He needs to know how to cry himself to sleep."

"I do not think that is necessary."

"Yes, it is." She grabbed the baby from her arms. James wailed as the woman placed him in his bed.

Veronika jumped to her feet and pushed the woman aside. "James is *my* baby, and I am your employer. You need to leave the room."

Mrs. Badeau's dark eyes narrowed as she stepped close. "Charles Fontaine is my employer, and he put me in charge of *his* child."

"His child is also *my* child. Now, leave before I fire you."

The woman smirked. "You can't fire me. You did not hire me."

Veronika pushed her away and screamed. "Get out!"

"I do not think my employer will like hearing that you have used force against me." The woman crossed to the door and then paused. "What kind of mother would be violent in front of her child?"

"I was not violent." Veronika stood there shaking as the door shut. Picking up James, she held him against her breast, speaking quietly, soothing him until he calmed down.

Why had Charles hired such an unpleasant woman? Since the nanny had joined the household, Veronika hadn't had more than a few minutes alone with James. Wasn't a nanny supposed to make life easier for a mother?

Veronika settled back into the rocker and cuddled James close. Why couldn't she leave and take her son with her? She could go back to her apartment and take care of him herself. Then again, Charles was the father. He did have some rights. Still, she felt like a prisoner.

Kissing James on his soft head, she relished the sweet feeling of hugging her child. His little eyes closed, and he drifted off to sleep. She kept rocking, rocking until her own eyes closed.

Veronika jolted awake and tried to get her bearings. Her arms were empty. She rushed to her feet and checked the crib. James wasn't there. She ran down the hall, checking each room until she heard a faint cry from the nanny's room.

Opening the door, she stared at Mrs. Badeau holding James. "Give me my child."

"Your child was about to fall out of your sleeping

arms. What kind of mother would do that?"

"A sleepy mother. He was not in danger."

Mrs. Badeau tsked. "I have called Mr. Fontaine. He is on his way here. He couldn't believe how little you care about his child."

"James is my child. And I love my child!"

The baby wailed as Veronika grabbed for her son.

The woman turned away from her. "You are an incompetent mother."

"I am not!"

"See, you are screaming. Disturbing a little harmless child."

"Give me my son."

"No. I was hired to look after Mr. Fontaine's child, which is what I am doing."

"You are a wicked woman."

"You are the one who has been violent with me, who pushed me away, endangered Mr. Fontaine's son, and is now calling me names. *You* are unfit to be a mother. Leave before I call the police."

Veronika stared at the woman's dark eyes. Evil eyes like she had seen in the past. Gasping for air, Veronika left the room.

How could that woman say those things and take away her child? What was she supposed to do? This should be the happiest time of her life. Instead, she was so frustrated and angry. She ran down the hall, out the front door, and sprinted to the beach. Faster and faster she ran, wishing she could run away from the past and escape with her son to a new life.

A crab darted in front of her, pincers in the air, ready for battle. All her life had been a battle, as she fought to survive, fought to make a life for herself and Deni, and now she had to fight to save her son. She stopped and bent over, trying to catch her breath. Waves pushed at her ankles; sand sucked at her feet. How could this be happening? Why couldn't all this only be a nightmare? How could she rescue her son from that evil woman?

She needed to call someone for help. Why couldn't Mikhail be a policeman here in this town? Why couldn't Deni be here with her? Why did she ever get involved with Charles? She knew he was an actor. Had everything about their relationship been a big act, a lie? Did he use her?

Deni would tell her to pray. Veronika looked up at the sky and wondered where God was and why he kept picking on her. A seagull flew down, aiming right at her. She screamed and covered her head. The bird swooped down and instead grabbed the crab. She needed to get back to James and think of ways to win this battle, take charge of her life, and save her son.

Twenty-Four

That night, Veronika sat on the plush couch in front of the stone fireplace of Charles's office.

Sending her a scathing look, he paced in front of her. "I was trying to finish up the film when I received a call from the nanny telling me that you are being dangerous and irresponsible with my son."

"*Our* son."

He shook his head. "You are accusing Mrs. Badeau of things I think *you* are doing." Charles's eyes went dark and cold. "You haven't been right since James's birth. I think it's been too much for you. I'm grateful she is here. No telling what would happen to my son." He walked to the windows, his back to her.

"That is not true. *Our* son would be much happier if *she* were not here."

Charles rubbed his forehead and blew out a breath. "Don't be ridiculous." He turned to her. "Veronika, you came from a troubled past, and I think your past has caught up with you. You can hide behind your new names, Veronika or Ms. V., but you will always be Nika."

Her heart hammered as tears blurred her vision. Shaking, she stood to her feet. "Don't you dare throw that in my face? I told you those things in confidence."

"Good thing you told me because it helps me

understand how messed up you are.

"*What?* I am not messed up. I have made something of myself. I love my son, and I want the best for him."

"No, the best for him would be for you to leave."

She clenched her hands into fists. "I am *not* going anywhere without my son."

Charles, at full speed, crossed the room and stood in front of her. "*My* son belongs here with me." His voice seethed, sizzling with anger. "Take time away, or I will throw you out right now. Come back in two weeks, and we will talk about the next steps."

"Two weeks? Charles, James is my son. How can you do this to me?"

He walked away, stopped at the door, and turned back. "I'll keep James while you are gone. Pack your bags, or I will have Mrs. Badeau pack them for you."

* * *

Six days later, Veronika sipped her fifth cup of coffee while waiting on the photographer to prepare the next shoot. She'd cried herself to sleep every night, and even when she had slept, it hadn't been more than a few hours. Thankfully, her client liked a model with a distressed look and dark circles under her eyes.

Every night she called to check on James, but no one would let her talk to Charles or give her an update. After the week was over, she'd go back and fight for her rights as a mother. James was *her* son, and she had as much right to him as Charles. The courts usually sided with the mother, so if it came down to a court battle, she would be ready.

Once the photo shoot was over for the day, she took the Metro to a little store to pick up a soda water to take back to her hotel room. She stepped inside and made her way to the correct aisle. A heavyset man stood surveying an item on the shelf. Something about him made her breath catch. She hurried past and stole a glance at him. He was the spitting image of the policeman who took her from the wreck where her parents were killed. Was he the man who had taken her to the horrible orphanage?

Her heart hammering, Veronika ran out of the store and did not stop until she was safe and locked behind her hotel room door. Surely it was her imagination. Maybe she was losing her mind. She sank to the floor and sobbed. Maybe she wasn't a good mother to her child. Maybe her past had been too much for her, and she was breaking down.

No. No, she had to fight for her son. She rose to her feet, threw her clothes in her bag, and checked out of the hotel.

* * *

Thankfully, the villa's front door was unlocked. Veronika slipped in without anyone seeing her. She tiptoed down the hallway to the baby's room. The door was open, and she peered inside. James wasn't in his crib. Steadying her breath, she hurried down the hall. Voices drifted from the family room, and she turned toward the sound.

Stopping outside the partially open door, she peaked inside. Charles, talking and laughing, stood with the baby in his arms. Maybe everything was okay. Maybe it was all in her imagination.

Another person came into view. The dark-haired actress from his movie, the one Veronika had seen in the photos, walked toward Charles and James, then wrapped her arms around him and the baby. "I'm so glad we're finally together."

Charles kissed her. "After this week, we'll all be together. Our wedding will be announced, and James will be ours."

Heart ramming into her throat, Veronika bolted into the room. "What is going on? Give me my baby."

Charles whirled around, his eyes blazing. "What are you doing here?"

"What am I doing here? I have been living here. And James is my baby." She shoved the woman aside and reached for the baby.

Charles blocked her. "This is *my* son, and this is my fiancé. You have no claim on my son. You signed away your parental rights, and your name has been removed from the birth certificate."

"What are you talking about?"

"You willingly signed away your rights to my son. The paperwork is filed and finalized."

"I did not sign any papers!"

"Yes, you did." He handed the baby to his girlfriend and pointed to the paperwork on his desk."

Veronika studied the papers. Her signature *was* on the bottom. She thought back to those first few days when she felt so sick and nauseous. Had he drugged her then? "You tricked me. You told me to sign the birth paperwork for James."

"I did not lie. It was paperwork for what was best for my son." Charles turned to the other woman. "See, I told you she was delusional. We've been letting her stay here while she recovered from her breakdown."

"Charles, you are too kind." The woman kissed him, then turned to her. "Veronika, you really should get professional help. Charles and I have been together for over a year. He loves me, and I love him. If anyone should raise his child, it should be me. I will be his wife in just a few weeks. You should leave now."

Veronika couldn't breathe, couldn't think. He was an actor. Was their whole relationship an act? He didn't love her. He had used her, and now he was taking her baby. She vaulted forward, grabbing for James. Strong hands came from behind her and held her tight. "I've got her boss." A deep male voice thundered behind her.

Charles addressed the man. "Take Veronika upstairs, get her things, then throw her out."

Wailing, Veronika screamed. "Charles, do not do this to me." She held out her heart—beating, needy, and wounded.

He turned and walked away.

Her belongings scattered at her feet, Veronika stood at the doorway of the villa and screamed at Charles. "You cannot keep me from my son!"

He stepped so close that she could see the sweat beading on his forehead and the veins bulging on the side of his neck. "You have *no* right ever to see *my* boy again." He spat the words so forcefully she had to wipe the spittle from her face.

"He is *my* son!" She screamed, pushed, and beat

against his chest.

He grabbed her arms and squeezed with enough force that she fell to her knees. "James is mine. You have no right to my baby. And if you ever try to see him again...if you *ever* come back here...I will have you arrested for trespassing I will call the police *and* the press and tell them you had a nervous breakdown from your alcohol and drug-induced lifestyle."

Her heart ripped into pieces, tears streaming down her face, Veronika stood to her feet. "Deni knows the truth. You will not get away with this!"

"Yes. I. will. Deni is your friend. Who will believe her? The others are *my* friends. They know my truth." His smile oozed confidence. "We have taken precautions to make sure what I tell people, they will believe."

"*Your* truth is a lie!" Veronika gasped for air. She couldn't breathe. This couldn't be happening. He couldn't do this to her and her son. He couldn't take away her baby. She had to find a way. Vaulting forward, she tried to get in the doorway.

Charles snapped his fingers, and the massive brute who threw her out of the house stepped forward and blocked her path.

"Take her away," Charles said. "Drive her back to Paris and put her back in the gutter where she belongs."

Twenty-Five

Music blasting and bodies gyrating around her, Veronika swallowed another drink and tried to focus on her surroundings. She'd been relegated to watching James grow up from a distance, finding ways to be near him by disguising herself. She'd gone to his soccer games, watched his school plays, and even found ways to leave gifts for him, leaving little wrapped bundles with a note: "From the one who loves you forever." As far as she knew, he never knew they were from her. She'd missed so many years, and only a few knew the truth.

She'd lived a good life the first few years after she left the villa, quietly hiring detectives to find the midwife who delivered James. The woman seemed to have vanished. Even wicked old Mrs. Badeau couldn't be found. Charles had covered his tracks well. Resolved to her fate, Veronika had fallen into a lifestyle of partying, trying to drown her sorrow over the loss of her son. The years had passed in a blur. Her career continued to do well, yet nothing filled the emptiness of her soul. Although she still saw Deni from time to time, they didn't have much in common. Not now.

Glancing around, she watched as people danced and partied, the others passed out from drugs and alcohol. What a fool she had been to trust Charles. And now, what a fool she had been to live the life he accused her of living when he took her son.

Rising to her feet, Veronika stumbled to the door. She was getting too old to party and waste her life. Maybe she would return to painting, find a house in the French countryside, and settle down. The thought of spending her remaining years alone ripped at her heart. Her so-called friends, those who hung around her, only wanted to use her for her fame and use her money for their partying lifestyle. Even though the distance had widened with Deni, Veronika really didn't have any other friends.

For all her success, she had nothing to show for her life. Maybe she'd try again to find the midwife or Mrs. Badeau. Maybe a new detective would find one of the women. Maybe now they weren't as well hidden. She stepped outside and hailed a cab. Eighteen years was long enough to grieve. James had moved to the states to attend college. She needed to change her life, and she would not stop until she reconnected with her son.

* * *

Eight months of waiting finally over, Veronika hurried down the hall. She opened the door and steadied herself.

Raphael, the detective she'd hired, stood in front of her. "I have what you have been searching for." Over six foot tall with dark brown, wavy hair, the man was handsome, and his smile gentle. He followed her into the kitchen and sat across from her at the table.

Hands shaking, Veronika took the paperwork.

"You'll find everything you need right there." Raphael pointed to the first page. "The midwife gave an affidavit that you are James's mother and that you were healthy and well when you gave birth. Charles paid her to tell others you had been on drugs. I also found the cook who worked at the villa during that time. She saw Charles put something in your water and food that first week. He had told her it was vitamins, but she said she saw the bottle. It was a narcotic. I'm sorry, Veronika. Both women and the other staff had been well paid for their silence and complicity in what happened. They both said the money Charles paid them felt like blood money. They said to tell you how terribly sorry they were."

Swallowing the bile in her throat, she turned to him. "How could someone do something so evil to another person that they would lose their child?"

"I can't understand their actions. I'm sorry. I can't imagine your heartache all these years. At least you have your answers now."

"Nothing can make up for the years I have lost with my son. I should have fought harder for him. Eighteen years I lost with my son."

Raphael's blue-eyed gaze surveyed her. "If I were James, I'd want to know the truth. During this process, I've been watching him. He seems like a good kid. I would be glad to approach him for you."

"No, that will not be necessary. I will need to figure this out before I make a move." So many years lost, so much time wasted, and now she had proof that she did not give up her son willingly. But what should she do with the information? Would telling James be something that would cause him grief? Would he welcome the news or be heartbroken that his father had manipulated and lied about his mother?

"You can call me anytime. I'm here if you need me. Veronika, I'm sure you hear this from many men, but I'd like to be your friend. You have my number, and you know where to find me. And Veronika, I'll be praying for you."

"Thank you."

After he left, she curled into a ball on the floor and sobbed.

Why would James even consider accepting her as his mother? Her career had gone well the last few years, but her jet-setting lifestyle overshadowed any success. What a mess she had made of her life! She was lost, adrift. If God was real, why did he continue to punish and torment her?

If she cleaned up her act, would he help her? For the sake of her son, she had to try. But how could she do that on her own? She needed help. Divine help.

The only Bible verse she could remember was John 3:16, about God loving the world so much that He sent his Son. She needed more than that. If God sent His Son, where could she find His Son?

Rising to her feet, she went to her bedroom and searched her belongings. Somewhere, she had kept the Bible Gabrielle had given her. She found the book in the back of her closet in the bottom of a box. She sat on her bed and opened the crisp pages. The page read, *The Gospel According to St. Luke*. She needed the help of a saint to guide her.

Time stood still as the words washed into her soul.

Even though the old English wording caused her to pause and stumble at times, she kept reading of Jesus, the man Gabrielle and Deni had said was the Savior. Her heart vaulted into her throat as she read of a sinful woman who came to Jesus, bringing an alabaster box of ointment. How she wept as she washed his feet with her tears, wiping them with her hair.

What had happened to the woman to be considered sinful? Had others used and abused her? Had others lied to her and stolen her child? Had she found herself in a situation where she had no choice but to live in terrible ways? Veronika held her fist in front of her mouth. How she identified with that woman. She had nothing to give Jesus. Nothing but her tears and her messed up, sinful life.

Ignoring her growling stomach, she continued reading. She had to know what else had happened to Jesus. She read how Jesus loved and cared for the people, fed them, and called them to be saved. Her anger grew as she read of His arrest, the false charges made against Him in the sham of a trial. Why didn't Jesus strike them all dead? Why didn't He show them who He was?

Veronika gasped as she read of his flogging. One of her acquaintances had studied Roman culture. She'd heard of the horrible things the Romans did during a flogging. The whip would have consisted of braided leather thongs embedded with metal balls, rocks, metal, or sharp bone. Jesus's back, buttocks, and the back of his legs would have been mutilated by the strikes of a Roman soldier intent on inflicting as much pain as possible. How could Jesus have willingly gone through something that horrible? Jesus was innocent of any wrongdoing. Jesus, without sin, was condemned by guilty, sinful men. Men who lied about him and abused him, yet Jesus willingly went to the cross and died for them, *for her*.

Realization washed over her. Jesus sacrificed his life *for her*. He bent over to take the strikes of the Roman soldier for her, for all she had done wrong. His back was shredded as though He bent over her, protecting her from the blows she should have received. She was the guilty one, not Him. Yet, he loved her so much that he did it all for her. He was the one who loved her, who loved her forever.

Veronika stared at the ceiling. "How could you do it, God? How could you send your only Son to save us? Our world is so terrible, messy, and full of horrid people. Jesus, how could you sacrifice yourself for the world, for me?"

As tears streamed down her face, she knelt and folded her hands in front of her just like she had seen all those years before when Gabrielle had prayed. "Gabrielle, Deni, and the Bible say that Jesus Christ is the Savior, so Jesus Christ, please save me. Oh, Jesus, I have made a mess of my life. I need your help. Thank you for the sacrifice you made for me. I am so sorry for the wrong things I have done. Please help me, forgive me, heal me, and restore me. Help me turn my life around. Change me. I do not want to do life on my own anymore. I surrender to you. Take my heart. Make it yours. Whatever happens, I want to be yours. Please show me the way to live. I'm all yours."

A soul-deep stillness washed over her heart, almost

like a cleansing from head to toe. She put her hand over her mouth, stifling a sob. She wasn't alone anymore. God was with her; Jesus was with her. Oh, why had she waited this long? Crying and laughing, she looked up. "Thank you, God. Thank you, Jesus, for saving me."

* * *

Veronika laughed at Deni's squeal at the other end of the telephone line.

"You did it!" Deni's joyful laughter thrilled her. "You finally did it! Welcome to the family of God."

"I am sorry it took me so long."

"Me, too, but I'm glad you finally made the leap into life."

"I like that. I made a life leap." Smiling, Veronika sat on her bed and curled her legs under her.

"Eternal life. It's the best."

"I just wish it would erase all my mistakes."

"Jesus washes away our sins."

Veronika sighed. "Yes, but our actions can have such nasty consequences."

"True, but things are different now. You've been given a new life. I'll admit it's good to see you sober and not in the papers with your wild parties."

"Life is different. So much better, and it is nice to wake up without a hangover or to wonder what horrible thing I have done in the night hours. I am scaling back my modeling and returned to painting again."

"That is wonderful news."

"Yes, now I am praying about what is next. Should

I stay in Paris or move somewhere else?"

"Move? Where would you go?"

"I am not sure. James is in the states now in college. I have been considering moving to be near where he is. Maybe one day I will contact him."

"I think you should. He has a right to know his real mother."

"I am unsure how to do that without making his father look bad."

"Charles is a jerk. I'm sorry, but he is. It was an awful, awful thing he did to you. I'm so sorry I didn't help you more."

"He would have tried to ruin you, too, if he could have. But, regardless of what happened, would it help James to know the truth about his father?"

"I don't know. That's one to pray about. God knows what's best."

"Yes, but I wish God would give me a sign saying exactly what I should do and when I should do it."

"I think we all wish that at one time or another. Keep praying. God will show you."

"Thank you, friend. I will never be able to repay you for your precious friendship over the years."

"The feelings are mutual." Deni paused. "I wish I was there to give you a big hug. Life hasn't been an easy road, but I'm sure glad you were on it with me."

"As am I. I will see you soon."

After saying goodbye, Veronika hung up the phone. Life was very different now in many ways. Yet, she felt that something else would come soon—something she needed to be prepared for. Whatever came next, her life would change.

Twenty-Six

Although she'd scaled back on her modeling and now only took more appropriate projects for her new life, the morning's photoshoot had gone well. Veronika changed into her regular clothing before calling it a day. She needed to pick up a few items from the grocery store on her way home, then get back to her latest painting of the French countryside. Spending her time in front of the easel had given her a relaxing way to spend her time. Plus, she had seen Raphael, the detective. They were just friends but having a good man in her life was pleasant. She grabbed her purse and stepped out of the changing room in the studio.

"Ms. V., do you have a comment?" A black-haired, thirty-something newsman shoved a microphone in her face with a cameraman behind him.

Veronika stepped back and glanced at the others around her but was only met by blank expressions and shoulder shrugs. She refocused on the man in front of her. "Excuse me? I am not sure what you are talking about?"

"Charles Fontaine died of a heart attack this morning. At one time, I know you two were an item." He rammed the microphone into her face again. "Do you have a comment for us?"

Head swirling, she turned away. "No, I have

nothing to say." Was Charles dead? A myriad of emotions swirled in her mind. Was she finally free? Was her nightmare over? But, then again, what of James? How would he feel about his father dying? She turned back to the newsman. "Wait, yes. Please let his son know how sorry I am to hear of his father's death."

The man nodded and walked away.

As though in a trance, Veronika walked back to her apartment. With Charles gone, she should be free to contact her son. But what would James say? How would she go about contacting him after all these years? What would he think of Charles and her if she told James the truth about his dad? Even though she now had proof of what happened, how would James process everything?

She opened her apartment door, stepped inside, and locked the door behind her. "Oh, God, what do I do?"

Twenty-Seven

With her pulse rocketing through her veins Veronika hurried through the misty, cold rain swirling around her. Her prayers were desperate. Today was finally the day she had hoped and prayed for all these years. Last week her detective friend, Raphael, had contacted James and asked if he would be willing to visit with the famous model, Ms. V. James had agreed to meet her at a little coffee shop near where he attended university.

She had prayed and rehearsed what she would say a thousand times. Yet, nothing she said seemed like it would be enough to convince her son she had not abandoned him when he was a baby. Even with the paperwork she now had, how could he understand she hadn't fought for him? Would the ragged ache in her chest ever leave?

With another prayer running through her mind, she stepped inside the building and removed her wet jacket. The scent of coffee, cinnamon, and warm bread welcomed her. A photographic mural of the mountains covered the walls. She made her way across the polished concrete floors. Two teenage girls sat quietly talking at a table next to the door. A young, dark-haired woman wearing oversized glasses typed on a laptop. At another table, an older gentleman sat with his head down, reading a book.

No sign of James. Veronika stepped to the counter and inspected the black chalkboard listing the café's menu.

Veronika ordered and paid for her coffee, then settled at a small table in the back and checked her watch. Hopefully, James would arrive soon. Heart pounding, she sipped her drink and waited.

The door opened, and James, wearing a black hoodie, jeans, and a blue T-shirt, stepped inside. He sloughed off his jacket and ran a hand through his blond hair. His gaze scanned the room, and a slight smile lit his face when he saw her. Hesitating a moment, he approached her table and slid into the seat across from her. "Hi, Ms. V."

"Hello, James." He looked like his father, yet he had her hair coloring and her eyes. Tears threatened her. She swallowed a drink of her coffee to dislodge the lump in her throat.

His gaze, curious, tender, and a little sad, studied her for a moment. "It's very nice to meet you."

"It is very nice also to see you." How she longed to reach out and touch him. Instead, she grabbed her napkin and forced her hands onto her lap. "May I buy you a cup of coffee or a pastry?"

"No, I'm good." He tugged on his T-shirt collar as though it was too tight.

Trying to think of something to say, she stared at the black liquid in her cup. When she looked up, James's expression was full of questions as he stared at her. She couldn't imagine what he was thinking.

She forced a smile. "You came here on a soccer

scholarship. Is that going well? And your studies, are they also going well?"

"Yes, they are both going well." He leaned forward, his gaze never leaving her face. "I'm enjoying college life and my classes."

"Good. I am happy to hear that. Do you like living in the States?"

"Yes, it's very nice. Girls here like my French accent." He grinned. "But I'm not playing the field." He held up his hand. "I have a girlfriend now, and she's really special."

"I am glad you have found someone." Noticing she had shredded her napkin, she balled up the carnage and took a deep breath. She needed to tell him.

A group of young men, talking and laughing, entered the café and sat at the tables next to them.

Veronika turned her attention back to James. "Would you mind if we continued this conversation in French?" She couldn't risk someone overhearing what she had to say, and she had no idea how James would respond.

He nodded.

"Thank you. James." Switching to French, she continued. "Have you been happy?" Her throat tightened as she said the words.

He tilted his head and surveyed her for a moment. "Happy? Yeah, I guess."

She gazed outside. The sky was now clear and sunshine streamed across the concrete floors. Oh, how she longed for illumination from the darkness of her past.

"I am sorry to hear about your father's death."

He rubbed the back of his neck and, for a moment, didn't say anything. "Yes, death is difficult, but it also brings discovery."

Veronika's eyebrows raised at his profound comment. She hesitated to say anything but now might be her only opportunity to talk to him. All the years she had waited and hoped to be reunited with her son. She took out the folder she had brought and laid it on the table. "I have some information that may be shocking to you."

"Okay." He sat back, a strange look on his face. Curiosity? Even humor? She couldn't tell.

Blood whooshing in her ears, she placed the paperwork on the table. "James, you may not be aware of some things that happened right after your birth."

"What things?" The question came without animosity.

She opened the folder and pointed to the affidavit. "I am your birth mother."

Without comment, without reaction, he took the papers in his hands and studied what was written.

Was he sad, angry, hurt? She couldn't tell. Perhaps he needed more information. "James, your father and I were dating when I got pregnant. I moved to the villa hoping your father would marry me and we could become a family. Unfortunately, he had other plans. While I was sick after giving birth to you, I signed a document Charles said was about your birth. I thought I was signing your birth certificate. I did not know what I signed." Her voice choked, and she had to swallow hard to continue. "I am so sorry. Please, please know I *always* wanted you. Oh, how I wanted to stay your mother and love you forever." Tears fell and she wiped them away with the remains of her napkin.

His head down, he shook his head, sniffled, and cleared his throat. Lifting his head, his teary gaze met hers. "You were the one who sent the packages signed with the one who loves me forever."

"Yes." She choked back a sob.

A tear ran down his cheek. He reached into his pants pocket. "I have something to show you." He laid an envelope, with his name handwritten on the front, on the table. "I received this last week from my father's lawyer. It was to be given to me in the event of my dad's death. I'm not sure why it took so long to get to me. But maybe now I know." He removed the letter and handed it to her.

Veronika's eyes blurred as she read Charles's admission to James of what he had done, the ways he tricked her into signing away her parental rights. He even admitted how he had kept her away, the threats he had made. Charles apologized to James for everything he had done, and he hoped that James would forgive him and reconnect with his mother. The whole horrible, sordid truth was now in writing.

She clapped her hand over her mouth to stifle her sobs.

When she looked up, James was smiling and looking at her with tears running down his face. "Hi, Mom, I think we need to make up for lost time."

Twenty-Eight

Veronika slipped out from under her quilt and knelt by her bed on the soft rug covering the hardwood floor. Her prayers remained the same year after year, thanking God for his forgiveness and asking him to redeem the heartache in her life.

Rising to her feet, she dressed and started her day. The art studio needed to be readied for the morning lesson with Emily. The young woman had been such a bright spot.

Veronika sighed. Even with all her mistakes, God had been far more gracious than she deserved. She quickly glanced at her clock and hurried down the curved staircase. Sunshine beamed through the windows across the hardwood floor. The room seemed to glow. When she bought the place, she spared no expense restoring the old house to its original pristine condition to use for her home, art studio, and gallery.

Turning right, she unlocked and opened the French doors leading into the gallery. She flipped on the light switch and ensured all her art was prepared for the afternoon opening.

"Good morning, friend." Deni peeked around the corner. "I brought over breakfast." She held up a white paper sack. "I couldn't resist picking up donuts."

"You spoil me." Veronika followed Deni into the

kitchen.

"Is Emily coming this morning?" Deni sat at the breakfast table overlooking the gardens.

Veronika sat across from her friend. "Yes, she texted last night to confirm."

Deni grinned. "Saturday mornings with Emily are always good."

"Yes, so very good." Veronika leaned back as she bit into a cream-filled donut. How grateful she was for God's goodness, yet how she wished things had been different.

* * *

Emily Lawton gazed out the studio windows at the meticulously landscaped gardens behind Ms. V.'s property. Even in November, the estate remained stunning and had even been written up in popular gardening and architectural magazines.

Emily sighed. If only she could capture real-life beauty on her own canvas. She turned her attention to her attempt at painting a field of flowers. Even though she'd worked throughout the morning, she couldn't achieve the light and peaceful mood she hoped to convey. Instead, the painting looked dark and foreboding.

"Gentle. Not too strong. You are trying too hard." As though reading her mind, Ms. V.'s voice came from behind her.

"It's frustrating. I can visualize the scene in my head but putting it on the canvas is hard." Emily turned and surveyed her tutor, friend, and mentor. Ms. V. might be in her seventies, but her silver hair, high cheekbones, and flawless porcelain skin gave her a striking, elegant, ageless, and regal sophistication. For some odd reason, she'd taken Emily under her wing when she was a little girl, giving her private lessons every Saturday morning. Emily never could understand the sweet, fun friendship she'd been gifted by the woman most people saw as extremely intimidating. Even now, Emily straightened her back.

"Loosen your grip. Don't make your edges so sharp and linear. Relax. Take a deep breath, release it slowly, and imagine yourself standing in that field of flowers. What do you want those who view the painting to feel? Often our moods color how we paint."

"I guess that's true. I'm kind of bummed today."

"May I ask what is bothering you?" Ms. V. moved in front of her, and her steel-blue gaze studied Emily's face. "You know I am always here for you. Tell me."

"I'm not sure what's wrong. Maybe it's the cold weather and gray skies. Then again, sometimes I feel like something is missing in my life. I'm not sure what it is."

Ms. V. quieted for a moment, then spoke in her soft accent. "Perhaps I understand a little of what you feel. We are all searching for meaning, purpose." She pointed to the canvas. "What mood do you desire your painting to convey?"

"Calm and restful. Carefree."

"Perhaps choose a lighter color here and here." Ms. V. pointed to several areas on her painting. "Also, make your shading not as dark."

Emily tried again, brushing gentle strokes and

adding lighter shading.

"Good. Much better. Remember, you can always paint over your mistakes. Don't be afraid to use your finger to add a slight blur around the edges." Ms. V. picked up an oil painting she was working on. "Look, I can wipe it off like this." She swiped at the image, leaving a streak in the middle. "Unlike real life, you can always start over." With a few strokes of her brush, she rectified the damage.

"I wish we could do that with our own mistakes."

"Yes, as do I." Ms. V. laid a gentle hand on Emily's shoulder. "You have no idea how much of the past I wish I could change." Sadness crossed her face. "I need to take care of a few things upstairs. Feel free to stay as long as you like."

Emily watched the woman elegantly glide out of the room. Ms. V. had been a successful model and actress until she moved to Springton, Tennessee, and opened V's Art Gallery and Studio. The reasons behind the change from her once wild lifestyle to quietly running her own studio had been the topic of many discussions in the community.

From when she was little, Emily and her Mom had spent most Saturdays in the art studio. Her mom enjoyed making pottery, while Emily loved all art forms. Over the years, Ms. V. had shown her how to paint, draw, design fused glass, make stained glass and mosaics, make pottery, and anything else she could think of doing.

Grateful for the improvements she was making in her oil painting, Emily studied her latest project. She'd sold several of her paintings but wasn't nearly as famous as other artists whose works were displayed in the gallery.

With a glance at the clock, Emily hurried to finish as much of the painting as possible and clean up her supplies. She then wandered through the art gallery and stopped to survey the latest painting from Lucas Sevforsen. No one had ever seen the artist, and his paintings were displayed exclusively by Ms. V. Most people surmised she received his artwork on her monthly trips to Europe.

The skill level of Lucas's work drew international acclaim, and his first painting sold at Sotheby's in New York for over $100,000. Lucas's works always had the same woman in a red Victorian dress as his primary subject. His first one appeared years ago with the woman crying as she stood in front of a villa with a suitcase in hand. In one of the windows, a man could be seen holding a baby.

Each painting had the same beautiful woman in various places around the globe, watching a little blond-haired boy from a distance. In one painting, he toddled toward his parent's outstretched arms. In another, he ran and played in a field of wildflowers. As the paintings continued, the boy grew in age.

Lucas's latest creation had the woman running in a forest as though searching for something or someone. Now taller and older, the boy could be seen in the distance.

Over the years, Emily had studied his work, noting the brush strokes and the realism with which he painted. Someday, she hoped to have as much skill as Lucas. It was a shame his paintings sold for so much money when Ms. V.'s works only sold in the thousands.

Moving farther into the gallery, she admired the selection of decorative pottery, many of which were made with the Japanese method, Kintsugi. She then paused at the four-foot-tall marble statue Ms. V. had sculpted years ago of the Biblical depiction of a woman weeping and anointing the feet of Jesus with her tears. The statue was displayed but never to be sold.

"Hi, Emily." Ms. V's friend and coworker who ran the gallery, Deni Allard, walked toward her and hugged her. "How's your mom, and how are you doing? Are you enjoying working at the law firm?" Deni, a widow, lived in a two-story stone farmhouse behind Ms. V.'s home.

"Mom's well, and I'm doing well. And yes, I'm enjoying working at the law firm."

"Wonderful." Deni's green eyes sparkled. "And...do you happen to see my grandson?"

"Yes, ma'am. It's funny now that he's a man and a lawyer." Brandon Thompson, Deni's grandson, worked in her building. Three years older, she always enjoyed seeing him on the weekend when he worked around Ms. V.'s property. Emily had a crush on him while growing up. When he'd graduated from law school, she didn't think she'd ever see him again, but now they worked in the same building.

"He was always a good boy, a little mischievous at times, but always a good boy." Deni softly laughed.

"I can imagine." Emily smiled at the fun memories. "I still crack up when I think about Brandon's attempt at moonwalking."

Deni chuckled. "The poor thing had scratches all over him from falling into the rose bed, but I think his pride took the biggest fall. He was always showing off for you. He thinks very highly of you."

Emily smiled as heat crawled up her neck. Brandon talked about her to his grandmother?

"Well, I better be going," Deni said, patting her arm. "I must run to the store to pick up a few things. Please tell your mom hello for me."

"I will." Emily turned to the broad, curved staircase leading to the second floor where Ms. V. lived in the beautifully renovated Victorian. "Ms. V.," she yelled. "I'm leaving."

A door opened, and her friend glided down the staircase. "Will you be back next week?"

"I'm not sure since it will be Thanksgiving. I'll send you a text if I can get away."

Ms. V. blinked as realization registered on her face. "That is right. It is the holidays." She placed her hand on Emily's cheek. "Take care of yourself, dear one. I..." Pausing for a moment, she then smiled. "I'll see you when you are able."

Emily hugged her. "Do you have somewhere to go for Thanksgiving?"

Ms. V. held her tight. "Do not worry about me." She stepped out of the embrace. "I think I will go out of town for a few days."

"Okay. Will you let me know when you're back?"

"Yes, and please tell your mother hello for me. I'll be in touch."

With a quick wave, Emily hurried out the door to her car and gazed at the old Victorian house. Ms. V. had the world by a string all during her younger years, but when she moved to Tennessee, the fashion world and

Hollywood forgot her. The quiet of art, small-town life, and her generous philanthropy in helping those rescued from sex trafficking had replaced her jet-setting lifestyle. Although Deni and Ms. V. were friends, Ms. V. seemed lonely.

Emily started her car and drove away. On her next visit, she'd give Ms. V. a much longer hug.

* * *

Veronika stepped away from the window. How she wished she had made different choices in her past, done things differently. God was gracious to forgive and welcomed her when she turned to him, but the consequences remained.

Turning to her computer, she pulled up flight schedules to France. The time had come to step out of the shadows and move forward, but before she did anything, she dropped to her knees and prayed.

Twenty-Nine

Brandon Thompson studied the estate documents for the Cowman family, ensuring the information was complete and ready for signing when they came in later in the afternoon.

He glanced out his tenth-floor window overlooking downtown. The law office of Webster, Ramsey, and King had given him his opportunity, and if he worked hard enough, he hoped his name would be added to the firm's banner.

After finishing his project, Brandon moved to the next stack of paperwork prepared for a client's trust. Hopefully, he'd have an opportunity to visit Alan in the law office upstairs. Then again, visiting his college buddy was merely an excuse he used to visit Emily who started working for his friend several months ago.

Brandon leaned back in his chair at the pleasant memories of helping around his grandmother's house behind Ms. V.'s studio. Emily had always been a little shy, and he loved thinking of fun things he could do outside the art studio window to make her smile. Every now and then, he'd even catch Ms. V. smiling. He never wanted to miss an opportunity to be near Emily. She'd been cute as a little girl; now, she was stunning.

He found a stopping point in his work. Ten-thirty would be a good time to ask Emily to lunch with him at noon at the little bistro down the street. Popping a mint in his mouth, he took the elevator to the fifteenth floor.

When he arrived, he stopped at the large conference room. Through the glass windows, he saw what he'd hoped for. Emily sat at a large marble-topped table, her head buried deep in stacks of paper, one as high as a small child.

"Hey." Not his best line ever, but sometimes just being around Emily made him tongue-tied.

A smile on her lips, she gazed up at him. "Hey to you too. Are you here to see Alan?"

"Yep, I need to chat with him about a few things, but I was also hoping to see you." He stepped closer. "Can I take you to lunch today?"

"No, I'm sorry." Her smile dimmed. "I have to run to the courthouse at noon."

Brandon hid his disappointment. "Maybe we could get together another time?"

"Definitely. I'd love to. Yes." Her face flamed red after scattering a stack of papers across the table and onto the floor.

Brandon tried not to laugh as he helped her pick everything up. Maybe she was as nervous as he was.

She fanned herself. "I'm sorry. I...I guess I'm a little lightheaded. I think I should have eaten breakfast this morning."

"You toned to go to the courthouse over lunch, and you didn't have breakfast? Tell you what, I'll drive you through a fast-food place, get you something to eat, and then run you over." He did a little bow. "Would you allow me the pleasure of your company?"

"Yes, please." Her smile made his pulse kick up a

notch.

"Hey, Thompson." His friend, Alan, grinned as he stepped next to him. "Stop harassing my paralegal. The office would fall apart without her."

Brandon smiled and held up his hands. "No harassment going on. Just making sure your employee is properly fed."

Alan turned to Emily. "Are you hungry? Can I get you something? I have a bag of peanuts in my office."

"Wow, that's big of you." Brandon chuckled. "Pay your employees in peanuts." He turned to Emily. "Sorry, we go way back. Used to be on the same debate team in college."

"Yeah, I can't get rid of him." Alan laughed. "He follows me everywhere."

"So, how's the family?" Brandon asked.

Dark circles rimmed Alan's brown eyes, and even his dark skin looked pale. "Twin babies are about to be the death of us. I don't think we've gotten a full night's sleep since they came into the world. Don't get me wrong...I love them, but they are time-consuming little people. Why don't you stop by and give us a hand?"

"Maybe? Just don't leave me alone. I don't think I could handle dueling bottles and diapers."

Alan shuddered. "You have no idea. Babies are great, but when they both need changing at the same time, or feeding at the same time, or anything at the same time, having six arms would come in handy." He stopped, gazed back and forth at Brandon and Emily, and a knowing smile crossed his face. "Sorry, I didn't mean to interrupt." He nudged Brandon. "Stop by my office when you're finished, and we'll talk about that case."

"I'll be right there." After Alan left, Brandon turned to Emily and smiled. "See you at noon."

Once finished with his meeting, Brandon hurried to the conference room. Emily and the paperwork were missing. He turned the corner and checked her desk. She wasn't there either. Had she already left? Had he misread things? Maybe she didn't really want to go with him.

"Brandon?" Emily stood at the far end of the hall with a folder in her hand. "Are you ready?" Smiling shyly, she walked toward him. "I had to get everything taken care of before we left. You sure you don't mind?"

"It's my pleasure. A guy's got to eat, and what better way than spending a few minutes with you."

"That's very kind of you."

"Of course."

They rode down the elevator to the parking garage. Brandon opened the passenger car door for her, then hurried to his side.

Placing his hand on the back of her seat, he checked to make sure the coast was clear.

"I saw your grandmother the other day. She is so sweet," Emily said.

"She's a special lady. She handles the business aspects for Ms. V."

"Whenever she retires, will she move somewhere?"

"Nope. Ms. V. deeded the stone house to Grandmother Deni a few years ago."

"Wow, that's very generous."

"Yes, it is. They've been friends forever. And after what happened to my grandfather, Ms. V. made a huge difference in my grandmother's life." He turned in at his favorite fast-food burger place. "I didn't even ask, is this okay? Do you like burgers?"

"Sure, this is great."

After they received their orders, he parked the car and turned toward her. "I'm sorry. I should have done better. We could have at least gone in somewhere and eaten. I was thinking something fast so you could get to the courthouse."

"This is good, really. I love this place and eating in a car in the parking lot is my idea of fine dining."

He chuckled. "Well, I guess you're an easy date." His face flushed red, and he held up his hands. "I didn't mean it that way."

"I know you didn't." She giggled. "We've known each other for years. It's funny to be nervous, isn't it?"

"It is strange. I guess we're not the same kids we were."

Her head tilted as her gaze surveyed him. "I hope some things about you haven't changed."

"Like what?"

"I loved the goofy stuff you used to do."

"Really?"

Emily blushed, and she quickly unwrapped her food.

Brandon, wishing he could think of something witty or entertaining to say to her next, ate in silence.

Emily touched his arm. "May I ask how your grandmother met Ms. V.?"

"Sure. I'll try to keep it somewhat short. They were together as kids in a European orphanage and then taken to a kind lady's house for several years. When

Ms. V. became a model and actress, my grandmother became her agent. Then Gran married my grandad, who was a widower with two young sons. She raised the boys and my mom. When Grandad passed away, Gran assumed everything would go to her. However, he had never changed his will after his first wife died, and everything went to his two sons, who had turned into greedy adults. They took the money, sold the house, and left her penniless with my mom still to raise."

"Oh, that's awful."

"It was bad. Thankfully, with Ms. V.'s help, Gran and my mom moved to the States. Ms. V. even built the stone house for them to have a private place to stay. I went into estate law to help others not go through the heartache my grandmother endured."

"I had no idea. Is that why you were always around Ms. V.'s place when we were younger?"

"Partly. I did have other reasons for being there as much as possible." He grinned as he looked her way. He glanced at the time on his phone. "I better get you to the courthouse. I need to run in myself and check on a few things."

"Brandon, thank you for everything."

He smiled. "My pleasure."

He drove to the courthouse, parked, and walked her inside the building. Then he stopped and pointed to the right. "I've got to go this way. Do you need a ride back?"

"No, thank you. It's a beautiful day, and I think I can manage to walk a block back to the office."

"Okay, see you later." Brandon grinned as he

watched her walk away. He wanted to ask her out for an actual date, but with Thanksgiving coming in a few days, his schedule was tight as he tried to finish projects before the holidays.

In the last few months, he'd concluded that being alone was, well, lonely. Sure, he had a great family, but besides his grandmother, who lived in the area, the rest of his family had moved to Texas while he was in college. His sisters had children, and their babies were the focal point any time he visited, which was great since his nephews and nieces had to be the cutest kids on the planet.

For the first time in his life, he wanted his own family. However, not dating anyone did present problems in that scenario. He'd had plenty of girlfriends and made many mistakes. After cramming a four-year degree into three years, then law school, passing the bar, and settling in a law practice, he reached his goal. When he returned after Thanksgiving, he'd ask the sweet girl with smiling, deep steel-blue eyes on an official date.

Thirty

Thanksgiving turkeys obviously came with an ingredient that caused sleepiness and made stomachs swell twice their size. Emily pulled her jacket tight around her shoulders and surveyed the cotton-rope hammock on her parent's front porch. If she succumbed to the swinging pendulum of bliss, could she extricate herself before dessert was ready?

She probably should jog around the block to clear her head and make room for pie. Then again, the few times she had jogged, she'd wound up with shin splints and blisters on her toes. Sports had never been her thing. Art was her happy place for enjoyment and fulfillment.

Wishing she had brought her sketch pad, she studied the dark golden leaves tenaciously clinging to the fall trees. Even though she only lived an hour away in the city, life was gentler and quieter here in the rolling Tennessee hills.

Her mom opened the front door. "Emily? It's chilly out here. Are you ready for dessert? Your dad's hovering over the pie."

Grinning, Emily hurried inside, removed her jacket, and surveyed her parents. Jamie, her mom, was slim and tall with brown hair and brown eyes. Her dad, Thomas Lawton, trim and athletic, stood six foot two, with dark brown hair and big brown eyes. Both enjoyed tennis and biking, and their tans lingered through the winter.

Emily sighed. With her blue eyes, blonde hair, and fair skin, no matter how she tried, she couldn't get a tan. Fifteen minutes in the sun gave her a burn. As a teen, she'd tried the spray-on stuff, but it only turned her skin bright orange.

"I've given you both fair warning." Her dad, wearing his trademark goofy, mischievous grin, held his fork and plate in hand as he circled the kitchen island. "In three minutes, the pie is all mine if you don't claim your share."

Emily giggled, grabbed a fork, and waved it like a sword in front of her dad. "Mom, quick, cut fast, and give me a bigger piece than you give him."

"You two are silly." Her mom nudged them aside. "I can't believe you have any room left after our meal."

"When it comes to pie," her dad said, patting his once-flat stomach, "there's always room for more."

"And speaking of more..." Her mom gave Emily *the look*. The look that relayed she was ready for her daughter to settle down with her own family. "Any prospective son-in-law on the horizon?" Her mom, in feigned innocence, batted her eyelashes.

"Well, I do see Brandon Thompson at the office. We even went to lunch together the other day."

"Brandon?" Her mom handed her a slice of hot, fresh, apple pie. "I always liked Brandon."

"He is nice." Emily blew on her forkful of pie to cool it off.

"Is he still cute?"

"He is." Emily took a bite of her pie to hide her smile. Brandon's big brown eyes made her heart melt. Then again, a melting heart probably wouldn't be a good thing. Interesting how a mood could change her viewpoint.

Her dad moved closer to Emily, his eyes sparkling. "You know that pie sitting on your plate might be happier with me. I'll be glad to take care of that for you."

Emily drew her plate closer and blocked his utensil with her arm. "I'm taking my time and savoring each morsel." She took a bite, chewing slowly. Her mother's pies were heavenly.

After polishing off dessert, her dad sniffled and gave them both a pitiful little-boy look. "Well, I guess there's nothing more for me to do here but go watch football." He shuffled toward the door, turned back, and gazed longingly at the remaining pie.

"Thomas Lawton, you get out of here." Her mom shooed him out of the kitchen.

He winked at Emily. "Works every time."

Her mom chuckled as she loaded their plates into the dishwasher. "He thinks he needs an excuse to watch his games, but part of my favorite thing is curling up next to him on the couch after a good Thanksgiving meal."

Emily smiled as she helped her mom finish cleaning the kitchen. Her parents loved each other and had given her a happy home. For that, she would always be grateful.

"These are your leftovers." Her mom pointed to a stack of containers in the refrigerator filled with goodies from the meal. "You probably won't need to cook for the next two weeks."

Emily checked the mountain of food. How many turkey dishes did her mom think she could make? At least she wouldn't need to grocery shop when she returned home.

"Are you driving back in the morning?" her mom asked.

"Yep, I need to get a few things done. I still need to update several forms for Alan before his clients come into the office."

"Working in a law office must be exciting."

"Exciting isn't quite the word at my level; for now, it's typing, filing, online work, and grunt research."

"You've always been a hard worker, Em. I'm glad you could get away for a few days. Remember, with Christmas coming, you need to give me a Santa list. Have you thought of what you want this year?"

Emily grinned. "More art supplies."

"As always. Your art work is amazing, honey. Someday you'll be famous so you can take care of your aging parents." They both laughed. "Ms. V. loves having you as a student. Did your last paintings sell?"

"Yes, every single one I put in the gallery has sold. Plus, whoever bought them paid full price."

"I'm so proud of you." Her mom hugged her tight, then stepped back with a mischievous grin. "You sure you don't want to stay and hit those early-morning sales?"

"Ugh. Once was enough. No more 4:00 a.m. wake ups to run in a store with wild-eyed women on Black Friday." Emily shuddered.

"You've got to admit we had lots to laugh about once we survived the crazy shoppers that year."

"I think if we did it again, I'd wear a flak jacket and carry a riot shield."

"Now you're talking about my kind of accessories." Her dad walked into the room and opened the pantry door.

"You can't possibly be hungry again," her mom said.

He gave her a pitiful look. "But my mouth got lonely."

Emily scrounged through the odds and ends drawer and tossed him a piece of gum.

Her dad sighed, loud, heavy, and forlorn. "Fine, I'll go back and chew this little, tiny, itty-bitty piece of gum all by myself on the couch. All alone. By. Myself." He whimpered as he walked into the den. "No one with me. All alone..."

Emily giggled and nodded at her mom. "I'll finish in here. Go spend time with your lonely husband."

Her mom embraced her and squeezed until her stuffing about popped out of her, which after a Thanksgiving dinner could be dangerous. "I love you, Emily Lawton. Don't ever forget that." Her mom continued to hold her tight, her voice quiet. "Everything we've done was because we wanted the best for you. Always remember I love you."

"I love you, too, Mom."

Her mom stepped back, tears pooling in her eyes. "And one more thing. Promise me you will *always* be careful."

"I will, and I am. Don't worry."

Dipping her head, her mom hurried to the other

room and snuggled next to her dad.

Emily leaned against the doorframe, crossed her arms, and regarded her parents. She'd never known her mom to make those kind of comments. Was everything okay? Why was her mom worried? Her parents weren't perfect, but she never doubted their love. They continued to act like newlyweds when they were together. Someday, she wanted a relationship like they had, but finding true love wasn't easy. If only she could buy a riot shield and flak jacket for her heart.

Thirty-One

Emily heaved her luggage up the outside stairs to her second-floor apartment and paused to watch two squirrels chattering in the trees. Even though she lived in the city, her apartment complex backed up to a nature reserve.

Suddenly, the hairs on the back of her neck stood at attention. She stopped and scanned the area. Was someone watching her? Hurrying inside, she locked the door behind her. Good grief, she'd never had any problems and was always careful. Then again, maybe she did need to be a little more aware of her surroundings.

After placing the goodies her mom had given her in the refrigerator, Emily unloaded her suitcase.

A bang at the front door caused her heart to jump and sent her scurrying to check the peephole. Her roommate, Wendy, stood outside, struggling to hold her suitcase and several grocery bags.

Emily opened the door and took the groceries. "How was your Thanksgiving?"

"Good." Wendy dropped her suitcase on the couch and followed Emily into the kitchen. "I ate way too much and played games with the siblings and their one-thousand kids. How was yours?"

"Great, but much quieter. Just me, Mom, and Dad."

Emily helped her roommate unload the groceries into the pantry, including bran cereal. How a twenty-four-year-old came to be that reasonable with her life choices seemed incomprehensible. However, her friend's stability made her the perfect roommate and friend.

"Must be nice having a meal without fighting for food." Wendy took a glass from the cabinet. "You would think my family had rabbit genes. Even if I was married, I don't know if I could handle more than two kids. I'll never know how my brothers and sisters manage with their broods. Groceries are high enough for one person." She opened the door to the refrigerator and smiled. "Yay, I'm so glad your mom sent leftovers."

"We should be able to feed ourselves for a month." She wasn't a great cook, but Wendy appreciated anything that didn't come in a fast-food container.

"So, how does your week look?"

"It's going to be wild." Emily leaned against the kitchen counter. Even thinking about Monday made her tired. "Lots going on, and during lunch, I need to run to the courthouse for work."

"Do you have time to spend with the hunk who works in your building?"

"Brandon? Yes. We do keep running into each other. I wonder if he's just being nice because we knew each other as kids."

"If he's smart, he'll continue to be nice to you." Wendy nudged her with her elbow. "Go for it. He's known you forever."

"I don't know." Emily held out her hands in protest.

"I'm a free woman. I have rivers to kayak and waves to surf."

Wendy stared at her. "You don't do *any* of those things."

"My point exactly. Maybe it's time I did. Maybe they're safer than taking a chance with my heart." *Good grief. Why am I pushing against dating when the idea of seeing Brandon makes my pulse rachet up to the stratosphere?*

Wendy shook her head as she retrieved her suitcase. "Stop being such a recluse. There are some great guys out there."

Emily followed Wendy into her bedroom. "Why do I have to date every man I meet?"

"Because you want to settle down and have a family."

"How do you know so much about me?"

"Because you read every decent romance novel on the market and watch Hallmark romance movies. And you're always talking about your mom and dad's sweet relationship."

Emily trailed Wendy into her room and watched her unpack her suitcase. Her roommate placed her neatly folded items on her neatly made bed.

"Maybe I just like decent and sweet things."

Wendy waved a pair of socks in Emily's face. "Fess up, girlfriend. You want to be married and have kids."

Emily settled on the edge of her roommate's bed. "It sounds so old-fashioned when you say it. I admit a guy would be nice, but a man or anyone else isn't the answer to happiness."

"True, relationships aren't the answer to our

problems or the world's problems, but you do need to get out more. You hardly dated anyone in college. All you ever did on the weekends was go to that art studio."

"I love art, and there are not enough good men."

"There were a few great guys at school, but you were too scared to date."

"Ouch." Emily stood. "Why are you so pushy today?"

Wendy straightened the comforter where Emily had been sitting. "Because I'm your friend, and I need support."

"*You* need support?" Emily studied her friend. Even though Wendy was five foot two and tiny boned, she was an avid rock climber and scaled over any obstacle in her life.

Wendy's grin was mischievous. "Kyle called me and asked me out on a date."

"Cute Kyle? The Kyle who works at your bank?"

Wendy nodded.

"He called you?"

"I gave him my number last week when I withdrew money for my trip."

Emily bopped her friend with a pillow. "You've been holding out on me. You only want me to take a risk because you're taking a risk?"

"Yeah. It's only fair. We can both take the heart plunge together."

"Heart plunge?" Emily put her hands to her chest. "Can't you use a better word?"

"Fine. How about heart leap?"

"Not much better. If I do leap, you better be there if the cord frays and breaks."

"I've got your back. Let's go for it." Wendy took the pillow and placed it back on her bed.

Emily moaned. "Okay, I'll do it. If Brandon asks me out, I'll accept. Now I vote we watch a movie."

"Good plan." Wendy finished unpacking and pushed Emily to the den. "How about *Braveheart*?"

"Ugh, too much violence. I want my heart brave but without any battles."

"Emily, it's time to be courageous, valiant, fearless, and bold." Wendy placed her hands on Emily's shoulders. "This week, we will move forward into the love battlefield."

Gulping, Emily said a silent prayer for heart protection and high-fived her friend. "Okay, let's do this."

Thirty-Two

Emily glanced at the clock on her work desk. She'd stayed late to make sure signatures and notaries were completed and each form executed properly for the Townsend case. Finally finished, she placed the documents on Alan's desk, then went back to work on the initial drafts for another of his clients.

She still needed to ensure the subscriptions were updated and the supplements added to the back of each corresponding book in the law library. Two of the older lawyers liked using something they could hold in their hands, while the younger ones preferred online information. Hurrying down the hall, she stopped and admired the books lining the library. One of her paintings had been of this very room and had sold for more than she had hoped.

Projects completed for the day, she returned to her desk and checked her cell phone. Strange. Her mom had called several times. Emily turned off her computer, made sure her desk was clear and neat, and then placed the call. "Hey, Mom, what's up?"

"Emily." Her mom's voice broke, followed by a sob. "Come to Harris Hospital. It's your dad."

"Mom! What happened? Is he okay? Is he...?" She couldn't bear to say the words.

"He was on his bike and a car hit him. Oh, Emily.

Come quick."

Emily grabbed her purse. "I'm on my way." Praying like crazy, she ran to her car. She couldn't bear to live without her dad. He'd always been there for her and loved her even when she didn't deserve to be loved. *Oh, God, please, please, please don't take my dad. Please let him be okay.*

How she made it to the hospital, she couldn't remember. Running down the corridor, she found her mom alone in the ICU waiting room. Crying, she fell into her mom's arms. "Is Dad going to make it?"

"Yes, I think so. He's pretty beaten up. But...his kidneys." Her mom's breath caught as tears ran down her face. "He needs a transplant."

"I can give him one of mine. I'm young, and I'd be a match, right?"

Her mom shook her head. "No, no, Uncle Tim is being tested right now. It'll be okay."

"But Mom, I'm probably the best match he has." Emily noticed a nurse passing by. "Excuse me, but could I get tested for a kidney transplant for my dad? Like, right now?"

The nurse stopped. "I can find out for you. Give me a few minutes, and I'll be right back."

Emily's mom grabbed her daughter by the arm. "No, you don't need to do this."

"Yes, I do. Mom, I love Dad. I want to help."

"No, honey. Please, no."

"Why not? It's the least I can do."

Her mom's eyes were wide and wild. "No. I forbid you!"

"What?" Emily broke free from her mom's grasp.

"That's crazy, Mom. I want to do this."

"No! Sit down. Oh, God." Her mom covered her face with her hands, sobbing. "I never wanted you to know. I'm sorry I never told you."

"Told me what?"

"Your dad is not your biological father. You can't be a kidney match."

"*What?* What are you talking about?*"

"I'm so sorry, Emily. I was dating someone else in college." Her mom continued between her crying. "When I got pregnant, he deserted me, deserted us, and I never saw him again. Thomas and I were good friends, and he married me so you would have a father. I'm sorry I didn't tell you. I just never thought you would ever need to know."

"Mrs. Lawton?" A doctor stood in the doorway.

"Yes." Her mom wiped her eyes and hurried toward the man.

He motioned for her to follow him down the hall.

Emily wilted into a chair with her back against the wall. *Dad isn't my real dad? Why didn't she tell me? Why would Mom keep something like that from me?*

Why did she have to find out this way? She could understand not telling her when she was a little girl, but she was an adult. It was crazy.

She'd been born six months after her parent's marriage, but because of her small birth size, she thought she was a preemie, or her parents had needed to marry because of an unplanned pregnancy. Either way, she *never* would have believed Thomas Lawton wasn't her real dad.

Then again, she didn't look like either of them. And

if she was honest with herself, even as a little girl she wondered if she'd been adopted.

Still, she couldn't imagine her mom being with another man. Her dad loved her mom, and he loved her. His genes might not be in her blood, but he'd loved her unconditionally. No matter what happened, or what might happen in the future, he would always be her dad.

Placing her hands over her face, she silently cried out to God and let the tears flow.

* * *

Unable to concentrate, Brandon turned from his computer and stood by his window. He'd sent flowers to the hospital, but since he wasn't officially dating Emily, it wasn't like he could just show up, could he? Rain drizzled down the windowpane. Above were gray clouds, below a gray street, and even most of the cars seemed gray. Since Emily had been on leave, the world had lost its color. Turning away, he headed to the elevator and rode up to see his friend.

"Any word?" Brandon stood in front of Alan's desk.

"I assume you mean Emily." His friend looked up from his work. "The good news is that her dad will be okay. His brother was a match, and the transplant was a success."

"That's a relief."

"If everything goes well, she might be back as early as next week. You know you can call her yourself."

Brandon stared at the carpeted floor. "I don't want to intrude."

"Seriously? You like her. She knows you like her, and it's obvious she likes you."

"You think she likes me?"

Alan came around his desk and placed his hands on Brandon's shoulders. "I can't believe I'm having this conversation. You two go all googly-eyed when you're in the same room. Call her. You've known each other since you were kids."

"True." Brandon squared his shoulders. "Thanks. I'll call soon. Yeah, that would be good." He thanked his friend and headed back to his office. Why was he feeling so insecure? He'd known Emily since they were in diapers. Maybe that was the problem. He still felt like a boy trying to impress her. He needed to man up and move forward.

* * *

Smiling, Emily said goodbye and disconnected the call. Brandon hadn't talked long, but it was sweet of him to take the time to check on her and her dad. Life was good.

She tiptoed past her sleeping parents. Her dad had fallen asleep on the couch with her mom curled up next to him. Even though he continued to heal and regain strength, he usually crashed after lunch.

Hoping she had a few of her art supplies squirreled away in the basement, Emily tiptoed down the stairs and surveyed the cardboard boxes neatly placed on shelving along the back wall. She rummaged through several boxes and located an old sketch pad and enough supplies to spend the afternoon drawing.

After the initial gut punch about finding out she had a different biological father, her mom finally told her the man's name was James. Even with the negative circumstances surrounding his disappearance, her curiosity grew along with the ache in her chest. Was James slim? Perhaps he was a big man. Did he have blond hair and blue eyes like hers? Did he love salsa as much as she did?

What if James was an underworld figure working for the Mafia? Or perhaps he'd witnessed a crime, was taken into protective custody, and left town to save his family. He could even be married and live in a house down the street from her. All those scenarios rattled around in her brain.

As Emily shoved the boxes back in place, something fell to the concrete floor. Dropping to her knees, she retrieved an old shoebox. Blowing off the dust, she opened the lid and stared at a pile of photos of her parents. Why hadn't she seen these before?

Emily smiled as she studied the pictures taken during their college days. The first one was them at a beach playing in the surf. Several more shots were of a group playing beach volleyball, sitting around a fire on the beach, and other random pictures of different people with her mom. She paused at the next photo. Her mom smiled adoringly at a blond-haired, blue-eyed guy standing beside her with his arm around her shoulder. More pics were taken with the same man. Heart racing, Emily turned the last picture over. In her mom's handwriting, the guy's name was labeled James Fontaine. Was this her biological father?

Using her phone's camera app, she took pictures to

keep for herself. Perhaps a little online research when she got home would turn up something about him. She returned the photos to the small box and placed it back behind the shelving. For now, she wouldn't say anything. But maybe...just maybe...she could get answers regarding her birth heritage.

Two nights later, since her dad was stable, Emily returned to her apartment. She typed in James Fontaine's name on her computer. Pages of listings came up for work-related job sites, physicians, authors, musicians, revolutionary heroes, social site listings, and obituaries around the country. No one seemed to match the man she was looking for.

She knew the college her mom attended. James must have also gone there. Even though she didn't know his age or graduation date, several websites offered to help find school alumni. It probably wouldn't hurt sending out feelers. She submitted several requests and kept searching.

Pausing, she stared at the website offering to reveal criminal records of men with that name. Would she want to know something like that?

Wendy came up behind her. "What are you looking at?

"I may have found out the last name of my biological father."

"Really? Did your mom finally tell you?"

"Yes and no. She said his name was James, but I found a box of old photos." Emily took out her phone. "Check out the picture of this one."

"Wow, you look like him."

"I know, right? Mom had written his name on the back—James Fontaine."

"That's a cool name. Fontaine is French sounding. You do like croissants and French onion soup."

"So that makes me French?"

"Maybe. It's possible."

"I suppose." Emily stared at her friend. "Why wouldn't Mom want me to know who he is?"

"It's complicated, I imagine. Maybe she felt ashamed. Have you found anything about him online?"

"Nothing yet, but I'm only getting started."

"Have you checked the social sites?"

"Yes. There are pages and pages of men with the same name, but I don't think he's a revolutionary war hero. Not knowing how he looks now or where he lives doesn't make it easy to find him."

"You could hire a detective."

"True, but I'm not sure I want to spend good money finding him. He obviously didn't want anything to do with me."

"Maybe he couldn't be around you because he's in witness protection, or maybe he's a superhero who went back to his home planet to make sure you were safe."

"Gee, thanks," Emily said, then snorted. "That would mean I'm an alien."

Wendy grinned and nodded. "Explains a lot of things, doesn't it?"

"You're such a big help."

"I'm here for you. Well, not really. I have a date, so I'm not really going to be here for you. But you know what I mean."

"Have fun. I'll let you know if I find anything about him."

After her friend Wendy left, Emily continued her search. What if James Fontaine had died in a terrible car crash and no one knew? A thousand different scenarios played in her mind, but she did prefer to know the truth. Or did she really want to know? She whispered a prayer that God would help her find out what *he* wanted her to know about her biological father. Maybe nothing.

Thirty-Three

Emily stared at her painting in progress. She had hoped she could create a tranquil scene at the beach. Instead, it looked like a hurricane had hit the coast and left everything in shambles.

"Can I help?" Ms. V.'s voice sounded next to her. Her mentor worked on painting a field with wildflowers.

"Yes, I'm having trouble with this one. I can't get him off my mind."

"Him?"

"My birth father."

Ms. V.'s eyes widened. She stumbled backward, reached for a chair, and plopped down.

Emily jumped to her feet. "Are you okay?"

"Yes, of course. I just stumbled. I...I...didn't mean to interrupt. You said your *birth* father?"

"Yes, but I probably shouldn't have said anything." Emily glanced over her shoulder. "Please don't say anything to anyone, especially Mom, okay? I need someone to talk to besides my roommate. You've known me longer. I found out Thomas Lawton isn't my real father."

"Oh my." Ms. V.'s hand went to her throat.

"I know, right? Who would have thought? The only reason I found out is Mom wouldn't let me get tested to see if I'd be a match to give Dad a kidney."

"Is he all right now?"

"Yes, for all he's been through. He's back home. He has to be careful for the rest of his life and take medication. So, the last few weeks have been scary and strange. All these years, I thought he was my dad, you know? Now, I find out some guy named James abandoned my Mom and me before I was even born. How could someone not have anything to do with their own child?"

Ms. V. cleared her throat as her eyes moistened. "Perhaps there is more to the story."

"I'm sorry I brought it up. I didn't mean to dump on you."

"No, dear. It is fine. Please, feel free to share."

"Thanks. I saw a couple photos of him. He was a good-looking guy."

"No doubt, since you are a lovely young woman." Ms. V. gave her a small smile.

"It shouldn't bother me. I have a great dad. But I keep wondering what happened to my biological father."

"I guess that would bring many questions to mind. Perhaps in time you will discover the truth."

"I hope so."

"Emily..." Ms. V. paused and laid her hand on her shoulder. "I care a great deal for you. Please know I am always here for you."

Emily smiled at her friend. "I know. I always feel better when I talk to you."

Ms. V.'s eyes were rimmed in tears as she turned away. "I must go upstairs. Feel free to stay as long as you like."

Emily sat back and stared at her painting. Maybe she should stop for today.

After cleaning her supplies, she paused in front of the painting Ms. V. had been working on. With the level of skill her mentor possessed, she had painted wildflowers that seemed alive and blowing in a light breeze. Emily moved closer and smiled. She could swear one tiny bee wore a too-tight yellow and black vest as he danced on top of a flower.

* * *

Cold raindrops pelted her umbrella as Veronika ran to the door of Deni's home.

"How did the meeting go?" Deni waited at her breakfast table with a cup of tea for them both. "I was praying hard that everything would be okay."

Veronika placed her umbrella by the door and collapsed in a chair next to her friend. "For the information given, I believe it went as well as possible. First, there was anger, much anger, then relief, but now there will be time needed to process. We will meet again in a few days and decide how to proceed." The tears she'd fought for years ran freely now. She laid her head on Deni's shoulder. "Oh, friend. What a terrible, terrible mess I have made of so many lives. Why did I not fight harder for my son?"

Deni held her close. "You can't change the past, but God's grace and forgiveness has covered your mistakes."

"Yes, for that, I am truly grateful. However, all the

consequences of my actions remain. How can Emily ever forgive me?" Sobbing, she closed her eyes. Would the weight of her past mistakes ever be lifted?

Thirty-Four

Brandon hurried to his office. He didn't want to be late for his appointment with Veronika Zabelle, aka Ms. V. The woman intimidated most people; his law clerk thought she had probably worked as a foreign spy in her earlier years. Even though her English was impeccable, he detected a touch of her foreign accent. Intimidating or not, she was his grandmother's best friend.

When he entered the reception area, Ms. V. glanced at her watch, then gracefully rose to her feet and walked ahead of him to his office.

He hurried to keep up.

She settled in the chair in front of his desk, her steel-blue eyes surveying his every move. "Brandon, I need to hire you to compile financial papers and be a liaison to deliver a series of packages to someone for me."

"I'll be glad to help with the paperwork, but do you need a lawyer to deliver packages? Wouldn't it be cheaper to have them mailed?"

"Yes," Ms. V. stated as fact. "However, my identity must remain confidential until the appropriate time. The packages are going to someone who knows me but does not know we have a connection."

"May I ask what's in the packages?"

"Each one contains information regarding her heritage."

"Heritage?"

Her shoulders lowered for a moment, then she straightened. "Brandon, have you ever done something that affected other people? Something for which you wish you could make amends?" Her eyes shimmered with unshed tears.

He nodded as a memory flooded his mind. He remembered one of the girls he'd dated in college. Nothing about that relationship made him proud. He had not been the man he should have been and not the man he hoped to become. God had been far more merciful to him than he ever deserved.

Ms. V. sat silent until his eyes met hers. She leaned forward. "I want the packages delivered to a young woman. Her father is my son."

Brandon tried to hide his surprise. Had Ms. V. been married, and when did she have a child?

She reached into her portfolio and removed a brown paper envelope. "I want you to not only deliver this but also wait while she opens and reads the contents. If she chooses to accept the package, the parcels will continue."

"Don't you think she'll be uncomfortable if I stay?"

"Perhaps. I'm asking you to do this for me as my lawyer and friend. Brandon, I know this is a strange request, but you are an honest man, and I would not trust just anyone with my granddaughter. She must *not* know where these packages are coming from until later. They are to be delivered every week leading up to her birthday. And if you are willing, the deliveries start tonight. I do hope you do not have plans." Her eyes held tender emotions.

He nodded. "I'm free tonight, and I'll be glad to deliver the package for you."

She swallowed and wavered for a moment before composing herself. "Thank you. This first package will contain several photos of her father along with letters explaining a few things. My granddaughter may not know my relationship to her, but I have kept a close watch over her since she was a small child. For my granddaughter's sake, we have kept my identity and the information about her father secret. Utmost secrecy is involved until the final package."

"May I ask why?"

"I do not know how my granddaughter will react to these discoveries. If she is willing to forgive and willing to see her father, we would like to use your office for the final delivery." Unshed tears shimmered in her eyes, and her bottom lip quivered. "Several recent circumstances have caused us to take action. Her mother and I agreed that my granddaughter would be told before her twenty-fifth birthday. How this progresses will be up to her. The last package will contain a substantial amount of money and bonds from my son, James, and I want her to have everything."

Bonds? James Bond? Brandon had to work hard not to let his hyperactive imagination run away. He searched through the papers on his desk for his pen.

Ms. V. handed him her pen. Her penetrating gaze locked with his. "Do *not* click it more than once."

Brandon imagined the thing blowing up in his hand on the second click or maybe a laser beam shooting out if he clicked it twice.

* * *

Emily perched on the edge of Wendy's bed and stifled a giggle as she watched her friend get ready for her big date with Kyle. Talking nonstop, Wendy moved with the speed of a hummingbird fueled by an energy drink.

Emily chuckled. "Why are you so nervous?"

"I'm not nervous."

"You've brushed your hair ten times and changed into six different outfits."

"Okay, I'm nervous. Kyle isn't only great looking, he's sweet." Wendy pulled another blouse out of her closet and held it against her chest while looking in the mirror.

Emily shook her head. "I like the one you have on. So, what makes Kyle so special? You've dated hunky, sweet guys before."

"Yeah, he's nice enough to meet my parents, but he still has this quirky, fun side."

"You got all this from your visits to the bank?" Emily asked.

"Well, my last visit lasted over three hours."

"How did he justify spending an hour with you?"

"He helped me with my checkbook because I couldn't get it to balance."

"You bank online. Since when do you use a checkbook?"

A red tint crept across Wendy's cheeks. "Umm...I might have wanted individual attention. And I also needed help opening another account."

"You already have a checking and savings account."

"This one is a six-month CD."

"I guess dating a banker does have advantages. At least you'll keep a sharper eye on your money."

"And I'll keep an eye on him." Wendy grinned.

Emily's cell phone rang. Stepping aside, she answered. "Hey, Mom. What's happening?" She paused, listening. "Yes, I know you love me. I love you too. Tell Dad hello for me, okay? I love you both."

"What was that about?" Wendy asked.

"No clue. Parents can be strange sometimes."

A knock on the outside door caused Wendy to gasp. "Kyle's not supposed to be here for another thirty minutes. No!" Although ready and fully dressed, she ran to the bathroom and slammed the door.

Emily hurried down the hall, curious to check out her roommate's date. She peered through the peephole and blinked. *Brandon?* Or did Brandon have a twin brother?

She opened the door and stared.

Brandon, still in his business suit, with an attaché case in hand, stood in front of her.

"Brandon?"

He cocked his head and stared. "Emily? What are you doing here?"

"You knocked on my door." She crossed her arms over her chest. "You aren't going by the name Kyle are you?"

"What?" Confusion crossed his face.

"Sorry. So, what are you doing here?"

"I didn't expect you. I'm looking for Emily

Fontaine."

"What...?" Stuttering, she backed away.

"This is the address I was given. Is she here?" He stepped toward her. "Are you okay?"

Emily stumbled to the couch and plopped down. "Why are you calling me by that name? Why are you here?"

"I'm supposed to deliver a package to Emily Fontaine." Confusion crossed his face. "That's *you*?" His eyes went wide, and his face paled.

"No. Yes. Maybe? I just found out my birth dad's name was Fontaine."

"Incredible." He stared at the floor and shook his head. "Wow! I had no idea."

"Why are you delivering a package? Most lawyers don't do deliveries."

Brandon straightened, composing himself. "This is for a special client as a special favor." He opened his attaché case and took out a large manila envelope. "Your grandmother wants you to have this."

"My grandmother? She died last year." Emily glared at him. "This isn't funny."

"She did?" He scratched his head. "Oh, no, I'm sorry, this woman is the paternal grandmother of your birth father."

"What?" Taking the envelope, she stared at the handwriting of her name. "Who is she?"

"That has to remain confidential."

"You can't tell me?"

"I'm sorry, no. But you can open the envelope."

She peeked inside and pulled out two photos and two letters. The first photo was a professional photo of a smiling, handsome man with blond hair and blue eyes. *The* James Fontaine. "My birth dad." Emily studied the next photo with her mom smiling at James. She turned the picture over. On the back, handwriting noted the date of the photo. They looked so happy together. Tears welling in her eyes, she held the photos in her hands. She had his coloring, his nose, and eyes.

Brandon gazed at the photo, then his tender gaze settled on her. "I can see the family resemblance." He plucked a tissue from the box on a side table and handed it to her.

Wendy walked into the room, gave a less than polite look at Brandon, then hurried to Emily. "Are you okay?"

Emily blew her nose and nodded. "It's the guy who impregnated my mom with me."

Wendy's head whipped toward Brandon. "*He's* your dad?"

"No. This is Brandon." Emily held up the photos. "He brought me these."

"You know her dad?" she asked Brandon.

"No, I know her grandmother."

Wendy crossed her arms. Her expression turned scathing. "Emily does not have a living grandmother."

He nodded. "Yes, she does. Emily's paternal birth grandmother."

"Your real dad's mother? Oh, wow! Emily!"

"Who is she?" Wendy asked Brandon.

"I can't say."

"Why not?" Wendy's eyes narrowed.

"Attorney, client privilege."

Emily patted the couch and handed the photos to

her friend.

"He's good-looking." Wendy's voice barely whispered. "Your mom looks great too. I wonder what happened to them."

Brandon cleared his throat. "Maybe the letter will explain something."

Emily studied the envelope. The address information had been blacked out, but a handwritten note on the front explained James had written the letter to his mother.

A knock on the front door made her jump.

Brandon stood. "I'll get it." He opened the door.

"I must have the wrong apartment. I'm looking for Wendy."

"No, you've got the right place. She's here." Brandon showed the man into the den.

Wendy hopped up and gave the newcomer a big hug and kiss. "Kyle, I'm glad you're here. Do you mind if we wait a minute?"

His big smile said he didn't mind the display of affection. "No, that's okay." He grinned as he sat next to Wendy.

Emily drew in a deep breath. The words blurred as she read the letter.

Mother,

Please forgive me. I take full responsibility for my actions. Please *do not* tell Julie what happened. I do not want her ever to know. I'd prefer she think I deserted her than to know the truth.

I may not be with her and the baby, but my heart will always be theirs. Promise to watch over them and make sure they have everything they need. If you are able, please send photos.

James

Emily swallowed the lump in her throat. James really did love her and her mom. But where did he go?

"Brandon, did my grandmother say what happened, what he did? Where he went?"

He handed her another tissue. "No. I'm sorry. I don't know.

She opened the next letter.

My dearest Emily,

Forgive me for not sharing this with you in person. When I learned from my son about your upcoming birth, I flew to meet Julie and help in whatever way I could. However, by the time I arrived, Julie and Thomas had already married and seemed very happy. Although it was terribly hard not to step in and make myself known at that time, I wanted to respect my son's wishes and did not want in any way to jeopardize your parents' marriage or your new life.

Please forgive me. I love you dearly.

Forever yours,

Your Grandmother

Never forget, God created your innermost parts; He wove you in your mother's womb (Psalm 139:13). I have loved you with an everlasting love (Jeremiah 31:3). And this is my prayer: that your love may abound more and more in knowledge and depth of insight (Philippians 1:9, NIV).

Emily shook her head. "This is a lot of information to take in. These people are out there somewhere."

"Yes. I'm sure it's difficult to process, but at least you know you were loved." Brandon removed another document from his attaché case. "If you'll sign this, I'll deliver another package next week."

"Another package?"

"Your grandmother wants you to receive one each week until your birthday."

"Why doesn't she give them all at once?"

"I think she wanted to know how you processed everything and ensure you were okay. I can tell she cares a great deal for you." He handed her the letter. "Do you want to keep going?"

"I guess. I mean, yes." Curious about the next delivery, she examined the document. Romans 8:28 was written across the top. *And we know that all things work together for good to those who love God, to those who are the called according to His purpose.* "This is interesting." Emily signed the area where her signature was needed.

Brandon stood and lightly touched her shoulder. "Are you sure you're going to be all right?"

She shrugged and half-nodded. How could she answer that question? She wasn't sure what she would discover next.

"I'll be going then. See you tomorrow at the office?"

"Sure. I'll be there."

Brandon turned to Kyle and Wendy. "Nice to meet you both."

Wendy and Kyle nodded. "You too."

On autopilot, Emily walked Brandon to the door.

"I'm glad you were the one who delivered the package. I don't think I could have handled a stranger dropping them off."

"I'm here if you need me." He took out his business card and flipped it over, revealing his handwritten cell phone number. "Call me if I can do anything."

"Thanks." She paused for a moment. "Brandon?"

He turned to face her. "Yes?"

"Please thank my grandmother for me. And tell her I look forward to meeting her one day."

Brandon smiled and nodded. "I'll let her know."

Emily closed the door and returned to the den. In awkward silence, Wendy and Kyle huddled together on the couch.

She gave them a small smile. "Hey, I'll be fine. Go and have a good time."

Wendy stood and hugged her. "Call me if you need anything, okay?"

"I will." Emily turned to Kyle. "Nice to meet you. Take good care of my friend, okay?"

Alone now, Emily stared at the photos and reread the letters. Should she call her mom? Maybe now she would tell her more information about James.

Emily dialed her parent's number.

Her dad answered. "Hey, sweat pea. How are you?"

"Okayish. Is Mom there?"

"No, she ran to the store. Can I help?"

"Dad, what if you found out information about your past you didn't know?"

The phone went silent for a moment. "Well, I would probably talk with your mom so she could help you understand. You can always talk to me. We're both here for you and love you very much."

She took a deep breath. "I know. Thanks. You'll always be my dad. You know that, right?"

"I have never been happier than being a husband to your mom and a dad to you."

Emily squeezed her eyes shut for a moment to stop the tears. "Thank you. I love you, Dad."

"I love you too."

"Dad?"

"Yes."

"I received a package with photos of my birth father with mom. And a letter."

Silence lingered for a moment. "I see. Want to talk?"

"I'm not sure. I'm relieved, hurt, angry, sad, and yet grateful. Still, it's hard to get my head around everything."

"Give yourself time. Do you want me to have your mom call you?"

"No, I guess not. Could you pray for me though?"

"Emily, I pray for you every day. Can I tell your mom?"

"Yeah and tell her I love her. And I really do love you, Dad."

"I love you too, Em. Always and forever. We'll be praying for you. God will help you sort out everything. Remember, we are here for you and will always love you."

"I love you too." Emily hung up the phone.

Just who were James Fontaine and her grandmother?

Back at his apartment, Brandon disconnected the call and stared at the ceiling. Ms. V. had been grateful the delivery went well and was concerned about how Emily took everything. The relief was evident in her voice.

How and why had she kept quiet about her son? Brandon shook his head. And why hadn't Ms. V. let Emily know who she really was? And why hadn't his own grandmother said anything? He speed-dialed her number. When the call went to voice mail, he left a message asking her to call him.

Rising to his feet, he paced back and forth in front of his couch. What had James Fontaine done that he didn't want Emily and her mom to know? Why had he deserted them?

Brandon ran his hand through his hair. What else didn't he know? Did his mom know anything? He stared at his phone but decided not to call her. No, he needed to wait until he talked to his grandmother.

One thing was for sure, whatever happened next, he would be there for Emily.

Thirty-Five

"I'm going modernistic." Emily pointed at the bright red swath across her painting.

"I see." Ms. V.'s head cocked to the side as she surveyed Emily's work. "Why have you chosen this art form?"

"Because I'm confused. I got a package about my birth dad, James."

Ms. V. sucked in a breath. "Oh? Is there anything I can do to help?"

"No, it's just strange. I'm glad to know a little more about him. He was a good-looking guy, but I have so many questions. And Mom is no help. I guess she doesn't know much since he left us. But he said in his letter that he loved her and me even though he didn't know me. Plus, I found out I have a grandmother out there somewhere."

"Do you find that troubling?"

"Yes and no. Why hasn't she come forward?" Emily paused. "What if she's the old lady who lives down the street from my parents who never comes out of her house? I only saw her once when she yelled at me for crossing her yard. Now that would be disturbing." She sliced across her painting with a black streak. "When your world tilts, there are so many questions."

"I am sorry."

"It's okay. But who would have thought? I mean, my parents gave me a great life, but I wonder how things would have been different. Then again, it's probably for the best. I'm grateful I know Romans 8:28."

"Yes, God is working all things for the good of those who love him and are called according to his purpose. That is a wonderful promise, is it not?"

"Yes, it is." Emily brushed an orange swath across her canvas. Somewhere out there, she had a birth dad who said he loved her and a grandmother who was slowly making contact. Her life had taken an interesting turn with many unknowns, that's for sure. How did Ms. V. make the changes in her life?

Emily gazed up at her friend. "Has it been worth it?"

Ms. V.'s face flushed. "It?"

"Oh, sorry. I mean leaving Paris to move here and start an art studio. Has it been worth it?"

"Yes, on every level." She smiled. "If I had not come here, I would not have been able to know you."

"Then you made the best choice ever." Emily waggled her eyebrows.

"I only wish I had been able to be more involved in your life."

"Aw, that would have been sweet."

"Yes, very sweet." Ms. V. was quiet for a moment. "Is your goal to continue working in a law office?"

"Probably not. It's satisfying on some level, but nothing like my art."

"If you could do anything with your life and money wasn't an option, what would you do?"

"Well, I'd love someday to paint full-time and have my own studio. Maybe I could tutor young girls like you've done for me."

"That would be nice."

"Yes. Maybe someday. I'm grateful you keep working with me to help make my art better. Thank you for all you do."

"Oh, Emily. How I wish I had done more and could do more for you."

"You do so much. I love my Saturdays with you."

Ms. V.'s eyes shimmered. "How I love them too."

Wanting to lighten the mood, Emily thought of her plans for the evening. "On another note, I have a date with Brandon tonight."

"You do?" A smile brightened Ms. V.'s face.

"Yeah. He's pretty cute, you know."

"Yes, I know."

"I had a crush on him when we were younger," Emily said.

"I thought so. He was always a nice young man and very handsome."

"It's funny to think about us dating now. Knowing someone for years but not knowing them is kind of a fun idea." She brushed a yellow streak across the side of her canvas and studied her painting. "Kind of like the sun coming up on what was once dark."

"That is a nice way of looking at things. Perhaps your discoveries will lead you to many new adventures."

"Adventures sound good. As long as they are wonderful adventures." She brushed green along the bottom of her canvas. "Kind of like hiking without all the sweat stuff."

Ms. V. chuckled. "Yes, I suppose."

"Hey, you two." Deni joined them and turned to Ms. V. "I'm making dinner. Stop by whenever you finish." Deni laid her hand on Emily's shoulder. "A little birdie told me you are seeing someone tonight?"

"The little birdie would be correct. I'm seeing a rather tall, handsome man this evening."

"Do give him a big hug for me."

"Really?" Emily turned to her and grinned. "A big hug, huh?"

A red tint crept up Deni's face. "You know what I mean. A platonic hug without too much touching."

Ms. V. smiled. "Give Brandon a hug for me too."

Emily couldn't resist. "What if I even kissed him?"

"Don't push your luck." Deni giggled, then playfully smacked her arm. "I trust you two. Have fun tonight. I better leave before I get myself in worse trouble."

"I better leave for home and get ready." Emily put away her things. "Hey, thank you for letting me talk with you. I always feel better when we chat."

Ms. V. smiled. "You have no idea how much that means to me. Go on. I'll finish cleaning your brushes and store your painting."

After hugging her friend, Emily ran out the door.

* * *

Veronika set the table as Deni finished cooking. "What did you tell Brandon when he called?"

"The story is not mine to tell. He can find out along with Emily as you let the story unfold."

"Thank you, dear friend."

Deni took a pan out of the oven with the casserole

she had baked. "We have had a long, twisting tale, haven't we?"

"Yes, and I am very grateful God did not give up on me. Thank you for sticking with me when I am sure I had the personality of a cactus."

"You did have your prickly moments." Deni grinned. "But, Veronika, without God and you, I would never have survived."

"I am sorry I was not a better sounding board when we were younger. I missed so much."

"You gave what you could. I understood. God blessed us with Momma G."

"Yes, she was a good woman."

"I'm glad she knew you gave your life to Christ before she passed."

"As am I. But, even if it had taken longer, she would have known."

"Yes. The angels rejoice when someone comes to Christ." Deni placed the food on the table and sat across from her friend.

"I can imagine quite a bit of celebrating took place when I finally came to him." Veronika laughed.

"Wasn't that the day we had a record snowfall?"

"Probably from all the heavenly confetti. How grateful I am that God drew my heart to his."

"Me too. This afternoon, I stayed outside the art room listening as you visited with Emily. God has blessed you with a lovely relationship."

"Yes, and how I pray what she discovers will not change things for the worse between us."

"Emily loves you. I think finding out who you truly are will only make her love you even more."

Veronika's eyes swam with tears. "Oh, how I wish I had fought harder when James was born. How I wish James and Emily had been able to be together."

"The past can't be changed, but the broken can be mended."

"Yes, I know that now. I pray God's golden grace will weave through the brokenness of my mistakes to create a beautiful new beginning."

"I am praying that for you all."

"Keep those prayers coming, dear friend. They are needed."

Thirty-Six

Soft music played in the restaurant background, covering the quiet conversations around them. Brandon glanced at Emily daintily eating her lasagna. He felt like a klutz as he tried swirling his spaghetti with a fork and a spoon. No matter how he tried, strands continued to unravel. Hoping she wouldn't notice his clumsy attempt, he stuffed the food in his mouth. Renegade spaghetti slapped his nose, leaving a streak of sauce on his face.

Emily giggled, and then a snort escaped. Blanching, then turning beat red, she held a napkin in front of her face. "Ack! I'm so embarrassed."

Trying not to choke on his food, he laughed and wiped his face. Man, even her snort was cute. "No need to be embarrassed, I'm the one with sauce on my face. I guess I won't be asked to join the elegant dining club."

"That club is highly overrated. I'm a member of the casual club It's easier on the pocketbook and much easier on etiquette."

"I wish I had known. We could have gone to a burger joint and eaten in the car."

"Sounds good to me. I'm just glad we have time together."

He returned her smile. She was so perfect. Before

his mind wandered how much he would like to kiss her, he stared at his food and tried to relay his thoughts with a change of direction. "I know I should know this, but...what did you study in college? We kind of lost touch."

"I finished with a business degree but also dabbled in accounting and law."

"What made you decide to work at a law firm?"

"Someday, I'd love to run my own business. I figure law is one aspect I will need to know about, plus there's a beauty and protectiveness about good laws."

Brandon nodded. "True. So, what kind of business are you thinking about?"

Emily sat back in her chair for a moment, then leaned toward him as though sharing a deep secret. "I'd love to open a studio like Ms. V."

"That would be great, and Ms. V. would love that. Why didn't you pursue art as a degree?"

"Because I like to eat."

He chuckled. "I guess eating is important."

"I've sold paintings at her studio, but not enough to live on yet. Want to see photos?" At his nod, she took out her phone and scrolled to find the pictures she'd taken of her paintings.

"Wow, your talent is impressive. I'll make sure to look for your work next time I'm at the gallery. Hey, if I gave you a photo, could you make me a painting? My grandmother's birthday is coming up, and I have an old photo of their house back in France. I'll pay you. It would mean a lot to me."

"I guess I could give it a try, but no promises. You might not like it."

"I know you will do a great job. I'll bring the photo to work. How about a steak dinner and dessert as a down payment?"

Her smile widened. "You got it, counselor."

* * *

Smiling to herself, Emily stopped outside her apartment and gazed up at Brandon. "I had a great time."

"Me too. It was nice to visit outside of work. Sure beats watching you through the art studio window when you were younger."

She grinned. "Were you stalking me?"

"Definitely. But since you now work in a law firm, I know you know your rights."

"Yes, I do." A cold breeze played through her hair. Shivering, she pulled her coat tighter around her neck. "Your grandmother and Ms. V. both told me to give you a hug."

"Really?" He stepped closer. "I knew I loved those ladies."

"I told your grandmother I might even kiss you."

"You did, did you?" His eyes sparkled as his gaze rested on her lips. "You know you shouldn't make promises unless you plan to keep them."

Emily swallowed hard and stared into his big brown eyes.

Putting his arms around her waist, he pulled her gently toward him. "You don't know how long I have wanted to hold you."

She melted against his muscular chest as he put his

arms around her. "Shame it took you so long, huh?"

"I guess that means we must make up for lost time."

"Yes, I believe we do," Emily whispered.

Brandon tipped up her chin and kissed her.

With her heart beating like crazy and toes curling in her shoes, time stood still as she lingered in his strong arms.

Thirty-Seven

Brandon took the latest package from Ms. V. and placed it in his attaché case.

She sat ramrod straight in the chair in front of his desk. "I am grateful you are doing this for us. You will stay with Emily again as she opens these?"

"I'll be glad to." He leaned forward. "Why didn't you tell me you were Emily's grandmother?"

"Oh, how I wanted to let her know." She wiped away a tear running down her cheek. "However, we did not want to jeopardize the good life Emily had been given."

"I can't imagine how hard it must have been for you all those years."

"Yes. And now, I hope and pray that as Emily discovers more of her story, she will be willing to keep me in her life and grant my son the opportunity to visit her."

"I pray so too." He meant his statement. He had been praying for all those concerned.

"Thank you." She paused, her eyes scanning his. "You did give Emily a hug for me the other night, didn't you."

His pulse speeded up as he tugged on his collar. "Yes, ma'am."

"Good." She smiled. "I expect you to be the perfect

gentleman, watch over my granddaughter, and continue courting her. Make sure you give her another hug for me." She winked at him, stood, and left the room.

He sat back in his chair and smiled. Had Veronika Zabelle set him up with her granddaughter? Man, he loved that woman.

* * *

Emily finished reading the letters from the next package and glanced at Brandon sitting next to her on her couch. "They say how much James loved me and wanted the best for me. He even watched me from a distance while I was in college, which is either nice or creepy. Wait a minute. That means my grandmother has been spying on me too. Oh my gosh, I come from a family of stalkers."

Brandon chuckled. "I don't think so."

"What happens if I don't want to keep receiving these packages?" Her life had taken such a strange turn. Why couldn't she return to how it was before she knew anything different? She was happy with her mom and dad, happy with her life, and happy with her art.

"If you stop, I guess this is all you will ever know."

Emily ran a hand through her hair, tucking it behind her ear. "I want to know, and I don't want to know. Wait, you *have* met my grandmother. Is she nice?"

Brandon placed his arm over her shoulder. "She is wonderful, and she loves you very much. And she loves the family you were given."

She nestled next to him. "Okay, so what if I only

wanted to meet her and not James?"

"Not sure. I think her goal is to reunite you with her and your dad."

"My *dad* is Thomas Lawton. James might have given me his DNA, but he isn't my dad." Emily stood and walked into the kitchen and stared into the refrigerator, letting the cool air temper her unexpected anger and confusion. She turned and looked at Brandon. "Wait a minute. Have you met him too?"

"James?" Brandon leaned against the kitchen counter. "No, or at least I don't think so. Emily, I realize this is tough, but I trust your grandmother. And, from what I understand, your mom was agreeable with how this was handled."

"That's right. I'm not sure how I feel about that either. Can I wait to sign the document after I talk to my mom?"

"I guess so. I can let your grandmother know." He wrapped his arms around her. "It's going to be okay."

Emily nestled against Brandon's chest and inhaled his clean scent. Why did life have to be so complicated? She had way too many questions. She needed to talk to her mom.

The next day after work, Emily drove to her parent's house. She'd called to let her mom know to expect her and that they needed to talk. Her dad was working late, so they would have uninterrupted time.

Bumper-to-bumper traffic slowed her pace, and she had time to think about how everything had been handled. She would never have known about James if her dad hadn't needed a kidney. She would have never known she had another grandmother. Plus, why didn't her mom and grandmother tell her everything at once, like pulling off a Band-Aid? Just rip it off and get it over with. But no, she had to find out bit by bit, pulling off layers of her sweet little, safely boring life.

Finally arriving at the house, she followed the tempting aroma of one of her mom's cakes, baking in the oven. It still didn't take away her anger. She threw her coat on a chair and stomped toward the kitchen.

Her mom glanced up from the cluttered counter filled with cakes. Baking was her mom's favorite hobby, but when she was upset, she would bake like crazy. Today, there were enough cakes on the counters to feed a small army.

Emily stood in front of her mom. "Why didn't you tell me sooner I had another dad, and why am I finding out now through a series of packages?"

Her mother continued to frost a chocolate cake. "It was best you didn't know."

"Mom, what did he do? He's not a murderer, is he?"

"No, he's not a murderer. James was sweet and loving, and we had talked about marriage. Everything seemed to be going well until he disappeared. I thought he just left us. It's been a blessing finding out he didn't have a choice."

"Because he went to jail?"

"No, not really. There's more to the story." Her mom sighed and wiped her hands on a towel.

"Not really? If he was in trouble, doesn't that mean jail? I don't want to wait for another package because I don't know that I want to know whatever I don't know from these unnamed people."

"Your grandmother loves you very much."

"Well, la-di-da, why hasn't she told me?"

"It's complicated."

"Complicated? How do you think I feel? My life had been turned upside down."

"I understand that feeling." She laid her hand on Emily's shoulder and pulled her close. "You know we love you."

"Yes, I know." Emily's anger drained away, and she sagged against her mom. "Way to pop my angry balloon. I was working up to start throwing things."

"You don't throw things."

"Yeah, well, maybe I do because my birth father was a troublemaker—a real bad guy. Maybe it's in my DNA."

"No, it's not." Her mom put her hands gently on either side of Emily's face. "I love you. Let's sit, and I'll tell you what I know."

"Fine, but I'm still upset." Emily snatched a fingerful of icing, licking it as she followed her mom to the table.

Her mom sat for a moment, then leaned toward her. "Here's what I now know. After a sports injury, James became addicted to a painkiller. Unfortunately, he wasn't using a doctor for his medication and worked for his supplier to pay for his addiction." She took Emily's hand. "When he found out I was pregnant, James wanted to come clean. But when he went to return the drugs and tell them he wanted out, a detective accosted him. The policeman told James they would keep him out of prison if he worked with them. James chose to help, which led to the arrest of a major drug lord and many of his accomplices. James was protected by his famous father and returned to France."

"Oh my gosh, he was a drug informant?" She narrowed her eyes. "That sounds like some lame movie."

"Truth is often stranger than fiction."

"You said he has a famous father?"

"Yes, the European movie star Charles Fontaine was his father."

"Whoa, I have a famous grandfather?"

Emily rested her head in her hands. She felt like her brain was ready to explode. Her dad wasn't her birth father; she had an unknown grandmother; plus she had a famous grandfather. Things like this didn't happen to ordinary people. She surveyed her mom. "So, why didn't James just call and tell you what was happening? Just think how different things might have been."

"Things would probably have been very different. I might have waited for him or flown to France to be with him. But if I had, you would never have had Thomas Lawton as your father. And I would have missed out on the wonderful years we've spent together. Oh, Emily, haven't you had a good life?"

"Yes. I've had the best life. But wait a minute, if James left for our safety, why is he here now wanting to see me?"

"Those involved in the drug ring are now dead." Her mom shuddered. "A drug war took care of that situation."

"That's too weird. Are you sure James didn't make this up to cover his tracks because he was a jerk and a liar?"

"No, it's true. James was, and I guess still is, a very nice man." The kitchen timer dinged, and her mom hurried to the oven and took out another cake to join the others cooling on the counter.

Emily joined her mom. "So, what's the deal with my so-called grandmother? She isn't that mean lady down the street, is she?"

Her mother smiled. "No, she's a lovely woman who loves you very much."

Emily dipped a spoon in the icing mix and tasted the sugary sweetness. "Everybody keeps saying that, but how can she love me when she doesn't know me."

"She has kept an eye on you from when you were a little girl, loving you from a distance."

"Again, that is creepy."

Her mom wiped the counter, then stopped. "Would you be willing to meet her in person?"

"Maybe. I don't know. You promise she isn't scary?"

"I promise."

"Does dad know her? Your husband and my dad, Thomas Lawton. My real dad?"

"Yes, Thomas knows her and likes her."

"Okay, I need time to think about this. I might meet her, but I'm still not sure about James. Would you be there with me?"

"Let's see how things go when you meet your grandmother."

"Fair enough. If I met James, I could ask Brandon to be there. He's a big guy. He could beat up James if needed."

"I don't think that will be necessary."

"You never know. So, why aren't you telling me the

rest of the story?"

"I know a few things, but not much. Your grandmother prefers telling you herself."

"She could call me or meet me somewhere. All this cloak and dagger stuff makes me feel like I've been...cloaked and daggered."

Laughing softly, her mom held her tight and rocked her in her arms. "I'm sorry. You'll get through this and come out stronger on the other side."

"Yeah, well, by the time this is over, I may have the physique of a major bodybuilder."

Thirty-Eight

Emily adjusted her latest painting on the wall of Ms. V.'s gallery, stepped back, and smiled. She was pleased with the landscape she painted of sunshine streaming through the branches of a tree-lined road leading to an unknown destination. Her work might not be the best in the gallery, but her skill continued to improve, and her paintings were selling at full price and even sometimes over her asking price. Maybe someday she'd be a famous artist or make enough to move on from her day job.

"Your painting is beautiful." Deni stepped beside her. "I think it's your best yet."

"Thanks. I appreciate your encouragement."

Deni gave her a side hug. "How are you processing everything?"

"With difficulty."

"I'm sure." She paused. "Emily, sometimes we don't understand why people react a certain way because we don't know their background and the facts regarding their decisions. Even in our own lives, we can't see the big picture. Only God knows the beginning, middle, and end."

"True, but sometimes I wish God would show us why things happened and if everything will turn out okay."

"We know we get a happy ending when Christ is our Savior. Heaven will be a wonderful place."

"Yes, but it's the in-between stuff that's a problem."

"That's for sure. Life can be hard, interesting, and yet at times beautiful." Deni guided Emily to the statue Ms. V. had made. "You do know what this is depicting, don't you?"

"Yes, the sinful woman weeping at the feet of Jesus."

"Have you ever wondered about her? What she might have gone through in her life, and what her background might have been? And what she might have felt as she cried over her sin and brokenness at the feet of Jesus—the one who was, and is, perfect?"

"I guess I've never thought much about it."

"Even though Jesus forgave her, people still knew who she had been and what she had done."

"That must have been awful."

Deni nodded. "Thankfully, God forgives us no matter how terrible the sin or tragic our backstory. Even though with Christ we are given forgiveness and a new beginning, there are often difficult consequences. It helps me remember to be patient with others because we don't know everything they've been through."

After Deni left, Emily stared at the statue. The woman had been forgiven and given a new life, but people knew she had been a sinful woman. Emily rubbed her chin. Did Deni share those things because of something she had done? What regrets did she have in her life?

Then again, what if Deni was her grandmother?

Please, Lord, no! She loved her, but that would mean Brandon would be her relative. Surely not. Surely Deni would have put an end to their dating, and wouldn't Brandon have said something? Still, she had to talk to him. If their relationship couldn't progress, work would be awkward, and a relationship outside of work couldn't happen. But how would she ever go back to just being his friend?

The next night at the restaurant, Emily poked at her food. Brandon sat across from her, looking all handsome and carefree while those around them talked, laughed, and enjoyed their meal. She'd practiced her speech for hours—what she would say, how she would react if Deni were her grandmother. Why did he have to bring her to another nice place? Pizza would have been fine with her.

"Is your steak okay?" Brandon tilted his head, studying her.

"Yes, it's the best I've ever had." She smiled and took another bite.

His eyebrow raised. "So, want to share what's on your mind?"

"That could be a scary thing, you know." With her brain in overdrive, sharing her thoughts could get messy.

Grinning, he leaned toward her. "I'll be brave."

Ready or not, she needed to know. She took a deep breath. "Do you ever wonder if there's more to your grandmother's story?"

He shrugged. "She's my grandmother, and I love her."

Emily took another deep breath and plunged forward. "Your grandmother is not *my* grandmother is she?"

Brandon chuckled. "No, she's not."

"Whew. It's not funny. I love your grandmother, but I was worried she was the one sending the packages."

"No. What got you thinking that way?"

"Well, I've known her since I was a little girl. And this morning at the studio, she said to be patient with people because we don't know the hard stuff they've gone through in their past."

"Sounds like a wise reminder."

"Brandon, what if she went through something horrible?"

"I know the orphanage where they were kept was terrible."

"That's so sad. I wonder if that's why Ms. V. never married. She always looks like there's something sad behind her eyes, you know?"

"Yes. Maybe her aloof exterior keeps people from getting too close."

"She's not aloof with me."

"That's because you're special." His eyebrows danced up and down.

"Right. I don't think so. I'm pretty ordinary."

"*Nothing* about you is ordinary."

His gaze caused heat to warm her cheeks. She took a sip of her ice water.

"Now that you know we're not related," he continued, "I think it's safe to continue dating."

"You make bold assumptions." She lifted her chin.

He grinned at her sly comment. "Have I made an assumption?"

She broke off a piece of her roll and tossed it at him. "Fine. I'll continue to date you. Only because our grandmothers want us to."

"I applaud your bravery."

She snickered. "I applaud *your* bravery. You have no idea what you're getting into, do you?"

"Nope, and I can't wait to find out."

Looking at his absolutely cutest grin ever, she fanned herself with her napkin before she combusted in a flaming heap of joy and relief.

Thirty-Nine

"Today is the day." Tired from pacing, Veronika collapsed on Deni's couch.

"It's going to be okay." Deni leaned over and hugged her. "You've prayed about this for years."

"Yes, but now everything may change. I have had the privilege of watching Emily grow, watching over Julie, and being involved in their lives, at least on some level. What if Emily does not want to see me again? My heart will shatter if she pulls away."

"I can't imagine that happening. Emily didn't have to come here almost every Saturday. She didn't have to share things with you and spend time with you. She chose to be here with you. She loves you, and I believe she will always want to be a part of your life."

Veronika put her head in her hands and prayed again for God's mercy and grace. If only she could go back in time and erase the hurt, loss, shame, and the many wasted years.

* * *

Praying, half-concentrating, and squirming between excitement and dread at meeting her mysterious grandmother, Emily made it through her workday and headed to Brandon's office. She bolted through his open door and perched in a chair in front of his desk. "What if she's a mean old hag?"

He chuckled. "Your grandmother is definitely not a hag."

"You'll stay with me, won't you? Please don't leave me."

Brandon's gentle eyes gazed at her. "I will never leave you."

Ms. V. stepped inside the room and nodded their way. "Brandon, Emily."

"Hi, Ms. V." Emily jumped up and hugged her. "What are you doing here?"

"Emily, I..." Eyes brimming with tears, Veronika dropped her head.

Then realization hit. Emily stepped back. "Oh, my gosh! It's you? *You* are my grandmother?" She fell back in her chair and stared. "All this time, it was you?"

Tears streaming down her face, Ms. V. knelt in front of her. "Yes. I am so sorry I could not tell you sooner."

All those years together, and she never knew. All those years, she was right there and never said anything. "Why? Why didn't you tell me?"

"Oh, Emily, I wanted to, but I never wanted to jeopardize the good life you had with your parents."

Emily stared into the face she'd known almost all her life. "Ms. V., knowing you has always been a bright spot in my life. I've loved every moment we've spent together."

Ms. V. clapped her hand in front of her mouth as tears rained down her cheeks. "I have always loved you."

"I wish you had told me. I love you too." Crying, Emily held her grandmother tight.

Brandon wiped his own eyes and handed them tissues.

"Please let me tell you what happened." Ms. V. sat next to her.

"You don't need to explain. Besides, do I really need to know?"

"I would prefer you learned the truth from me." Ms. V. stared off into the distance. "When I became pregnant with your father, I did not think I would be a good mother. I worried about my career; I worried that my baby's father would not want me to keep James. I was not married to Charles, and he often traveled with his work. When I told him, he was initially upset but then seemed excited. I moved in with him until James was born. We kept the news about my pregnancy and delivery out of the press.

"Then I left on a modeling assignment in Italy. When I returned, I found out Charles had been involved in another relationship for over a year. While I was gone, the woman moved in and had taken my baby as her own." She paused as a sob broke free. "I was shocked, hurt, and wounded. I left. Charles married his lover, and they adopted James as their own."

"You left your own child?"

"Emily, I did not believe I had a choice. Many things were happening that caused me to leave James in the care of his father. Many things I could not control."

Emily took a deep breath and slowly exhaled. How could Ms. V. have lived with all those secrets?

"After Charles died, James and I were able to reunite."

"You missed out on most of his life. What did he say when he found out?"

"He found out through a letter his father left him in his will. I met with James the next week."

"Wow, that must have been hard."

"It was hard and beautiful. God has blessed us with a wonderful relationship."

"Mom told me what happened and why he had to return to France."

"James is very sorry for the wrong he did and that he was unable to be part of your life, as am I. I am so sorry, Emily."

"I had a great life Ms. V. Thomas Lawton has been and continues to be a wonderful dad."

"Yes, God picked well for you in that department." Veronika gazed at Emily. "Now, my questions are..." Ms. V. swallowed hard, her breath catching. "Can you forgive me, and can you forgive your father?" She rose to her feet. "Take your time in answering. Whatever you decide, please know I love you." Abruptly, the older woman left the room.

Emily stared at the floor, trying to understand all she had been told.

Brandon hurried to sit with her and pulled her close.

She leaned against him, closed her eyes, and prayed silently. What was in Ms. V.'s past that she didn't think she was worthy of being a mother and left her child with another woman to raise? What would cause someone to do that?

The conversation Deni shared came to mind. Most people had a past they didn't want to share. Everyone had messed up in one way or another. Even people who took pride in their lives were sinners *because* of their pride. Without God's grace and forgiveness, no one would have a chance in this world. Ms. V. always donated her time to others—to charities, especially her philanthropic work with organizations against sex trafficking. Emily sucked in a breath. Was Ms. V. trafficked as a child?

"Do you want to talk?" Brandon's gentle voice drew her back from her thoughts.

"I'm praying for what to think. I don't know all she went through."

"No, I'm not sure we'll ever know all her story."

Emily moved to stand by the window and gazed at the sky. The years replayed in her mind. Every Saturday, Ms. V. taught her art, listened to her stories, and even attended school functions, quietly watching from the sidelines of Emily's life. She showed her love, waiting, hoping one day she could say something.

"Brandon, she must have moved here and given up her career to be near us. I can't imagine how hard it was for her not to say anything. How could she have done that? I feel so sorry for her."

"There's no doubt Ms. V. loves you."

"Yes. I can't imagine what my life would have been without her. I love her too. I never thought I could tell her." Emily smiled. "She's pretty intimidating."

"I know. But with you, she's always shown such a

gentle side."

"I've always felt a little special that I got to be around her. Now knowing she's my grandmother is strange. Of course, that means I have a movie star grandfather and a famous model grandmother. Who would have thought?"

"Pretty cool, huh? So, have you forgiven Ms. V.?"

"Of course. How could I be angry at her? Knowing who she is and about James, my biological father and her son... It feels like a weight has been lifted."

"What about him? Can you forgive James?"

"I hate what happened to my mom, thinking she had been deserted by him. That must have been terrible. But Thomas Lawton is an awesome husband to her and a wonderful dad to me. I've been blessed. I'm not sure James needs my forgiveness, but yes, I forgive him. Not any of us are perfect."

"Do you want me to let Ms. V. know?"

"No, let me go talk to her. She seemed so sad and worried."

Brandon cupped her face in his hands. "I know we haven't officially dated more than a few times, but we've known each other for years. I love you, Emily." Before she could respond, he leaned toward her and kissed her, a soft brush of his lips against hers.

She gazed into his big, brown, tender eyes. "I love you too." She watched as his eyes softened. He smiled at her.

Brandon laced his fingers in hers. "I'm sorry. I shouldn't have said that after receiving such a shock. Please forgive me."

"Are you kidding? You can't take it back now." She

planted a kiss on his lips to let him know she wasn't going anywhere.

A few minutes later, Emily floated to her car and drove to Ms. V.'s house. She couldn't believe all the changes in her life. She'd found out Thomas Lawton wasn't her birth dad; James Fontaine was her real dad; Ms. V. was her grandmother; the famous French actor Charles Fontaine was her grandfather; and Brandon loved her. Life had become a wild, crazy, strange, and amazing adventure.

She arrived at Ms. V.'s Victorian house and ran through the front door. She searched through the art room, the kitchen, the downstairs living area, and the gallery. A new painting by Lucas Sevforsen caused her to stop. The woman in the painting was now older, wearing a white dress and hugging the boy, now turned man. Down a golden road, a smiling little girl ran toward them both. Emily leaned closer. The little girl looked just like her.

"Emily." Ms. V's voice came from behind her.

She whirled to face her. "It was *you*. You're Lucas Sevforsen?"

"Yes. Like the woman in the story told in Luke 7:47, I was an outsider, an outcast sinful woman in need of grace. How grateful I am that my *many* sins have been forgiven. Now, I can see how God weaved his loving, golden healing and redemption throughout my life."

Emily reached out and hugged Veronika with her all her might. "You are my grandmother. I love you so much."

Ms. V. laughed and cried. "I love you, too, little one."

"What do I call you? Grandmother, Mimi, Mawmaw, Grand Momma, or just Ms. V.?"

"Emily, you call me whatever you want." She pulled back and gazed at her face. "Can you ever forgive me?"

"Of course."

Her eyes pleaded. "And James, will you forgive him?"

"Yes." Emily nodded. "I can't imagine how hard it has been for you both. Thank you for being part of my life."

Ms. V. hugged her until she thought she'd pass out, then stepped back. "Will you come early this weekend? I have a surprise for you."

Emily chuckled. "I wouldn't miss it for the world."

On Saturday morning, Emily sat next to Ms. V. in her bank manager's office. The balding, heavy-set man opened a folder on his desk and pointed to areas for Emily to put her signature.

Emily turned to her grandmother. "What is this for?"

"Trust me." Her blue-gray eyes sparkled.

Emily signed and handed the papers back to the man.

"Would you mind leaving us for a moment," Ms. V. addressed the man.

Once he left, she handed Emily a folder. "Inside is the deed to the art studio and bonds your father wanted you to have that he bought when you were born. The paperwork you signed will give you access to one of my accounts containing $100,000 to start your new life."

"What?" Emily sucked in a breath. "I...I can't

believe this. Oh, my goodness, how generous. You don't need to do this. I'm just glad you're my grandmother."

With tears in her eyes, Ms. V. smiled. "I want to do this for you. And, if you are willing, Deni and I will live in the stone house and remain as your helpers."

"I wouldn't have it any other way."

"And there is one more thing." She paused. "I would very much like you to continue seeing Brandon."

"Hmm. I don't know about that." Emily couldn't hide her smile. "That's a tough one, but I'll make the sacrifice for you."

Ms. V. grinned. "There is one more thing." Ms. V. stood and opened the door.

A blond-haired man stepped inside the room. His steel-blue eyes shimmered as he walked toward her.

Ms. V. placed her hand on his shoulder. "Emily, I would like to introduce you to your father, James Fontaine."

Light-headed, she rose to her feet and held out her hand. "Nice to meet you." Although he still looked like the young man she'd seen in photos, James had aged beyond his years.

He grasped her hand and turned to his mother. "She's lovely, so very lovely." Turning his gaze to Emily, he smiled as tears ran down his face. "I am sorry I was not there for you. Please, please forgive me."

"You're forgiven. I have been blessed with a good life."

"I am grateful. So very grateful." He gulped hard and backed away. "I will not intrude further in your life unless you want me to. Perhaps someday you will come to visit me at my villa in France? I would pay, and my mother could accompany you and any friend you would like."

"I've never traveled internationally."

He nodded. "I understand."

"But I would like to."

His chin quivered as he smiled. "You are always welcome in my home."

He looked so broken, sad, and lonely. Emily stepped toward him. "May I hug you?"

"Yes." His tears flowed as he gave her a gentle embrace.

She rested her head on his shoulder and inhaled his clean scent as Ms. V. moved close and embraced them in her arms.

Forty

Veronika smiled as she gazed out the stone house window and knelt by her bedside, praying and thanking God for her many blessings.

As the sun rose, she hurried to the kitchen, prepared breakfast for her friend, and then made her way across the garden grounds. Flowers and roses in full bloom graced the air with lovely fragrances.

Veronika unlocked the gallery's backdoor, stepped inside, and flipped on the lights. Making sure everything was ready for the day, she walked down the hall and stopped to listen. The sounds of life humming through the old Victorian house warmed her heart.

"Thomas James Thompson. Please get off the banister before you get hurt." Emily's voice came from the front hallway.

"Aw, Mom. I was just having fun."

Veronika chuckled as she watched from the entrance to the gallery. The boy's mischievous smile reminded her of Brandon's. Since he had turned six, Brandon and Emily's son had become quite the daredevil.

"Get your suitcase and make sure you help your sister with hers," Emily said.

Thomas heaved a dramatic sigh as he turned and ran up the stairs into Isabella's room.

"Honey, do you have the tickets and the passports in your purse?" Brandon stuck his head out from the kitchen.

"Yes, I have everything. Do you have snacks for the kids?"

He walked toward Emily, carrying a sack full of goodies. "Got the feed bag for the little munchkins right here."

"For the kids or for you?" She grinned and brushed crumbs from Brandon's face.

"Okay, some of it is for me. France is a long way. Man, I'm looking forward to another vacation. It's good to know Alan will take care of everything at the office while we're gone."

"I'm glad you and Alan opened a practice here in town." Emily stared up at Brandon. "And I can't wait to get away again. James's villa has been such a nice escape. It's so beautiful there."

"Yeah, sure made for a wonderful honeymoon too." His kiss made her giggle.

Veronika cleared her throat. "Sorry to interrupt." Grinning, she came around the corner of the gallery. "Go and have a wonderful time. Deni and I will take care of everything here. And please give my love to James."

Emily hugged her. "We will. He said you need to come and visit him next time. You know, he's dating a lady. Did he send you a picture?" Emily held up her phone to show her the photo he had sent. "She's very attractive."

"James did tell me about her. I do hope everything works well for him." She was grateful that he seemed happy now, settled, more at home with himself and others.

"So, are you and Deni going to behave?" Emily raised an eyebrow. "You're known to get in trouble when we leave town."

In mock horror, Veronika gasped and placed her hand on her chest. "Whatever do you mean?" She couldn't deny she and Deni had hired men to construct a castle playhouse complete with moat the last time Emily and Brandon had gone away on a trip.

Dragging little suitcases behind them, the kids tumbled down the stairs and vaulted into Veronika's arms.

"We will miss you." Isabella clung to her.

Veronika knelt in front of the children and hugged them close. "I will miss you both too. When you get home, we can work on another art project." How she loved these kids. Isabella loved to paint, and Thomas enjoyed anything that got his hands dirty.

"Will you make us another book like the bee book you and Grandmother Deni made?" Thomas asked.

"Yes, and I think we will write a book about a little bunny rabbit when you get home. Now, you be good for your mommy and daddy and tell Poppa James hello for me."

"We will." Isabella held her hand. "Will you come with us next time?"

"Yes, I will. I promise."

Brandon placed his arm around Emily's waist. "You ready to go?"

"Yes." She turned to Ms. V. and hugged her tight. "We'll text you when we get there. I love you."

"I love you all."

Brandon also embraced her. "Be good, Ms. V."

She grinned and winked. "But of course." Standing at the front doorway, she waved as her family drove away. Veronika gazed upward as gratitude swelled inside her. Never would she have imagined God could redeem and restore all she had lost as a little girl and the years lost with her son. The devil had tried to destroy the canvas of her life, but God's mending had created a beautiful masterpiece.

Dear Reader

I started writing this book in 2011 as a sweet romance between Emily and Brandon, yet the grandmother kept coming to mind, and I wondered about her backstory.

As God unfolded her past, I at first balked at the idea of dealing with such a hard and sad subject. Yet, those difficulties are real for many people. Terrible things happen and evil exists, which often causes a chain reaction of heartache and pain.

Our Savior Jesus Christ understands suffering. He was ostracized, falsely accused, mocked, beaten, and yet willingly sacrificed Himself in our place for our sins. He tenderly reaches out to those who are lost, forgiving the sinner, and offering new life.

God is a good God. Even though evil abounds in our world, what is done in the darkness will come to light, and evil will be judged. I've had my share of difficulties, and even though my attackers have not experienced human judgment, God has redeemed what the enemy has stolen from me. God will righteously judge those who have done wrong. St. Augustine wrote, "In my deepest wound, I saw Your glory, and it dazzled me."

God weeps with us during hardships. He is near to the brokenhearted. He binds up our wounds and saves those who are crushed in spirit. He releases the captives and sets free the prisoners, for He is the God of all comfort. (See Psalm 34:18, Psalm 147:3, Isaiah 61:1-2, and 2 Corinthians 1:3.)

Your life canvas may have been smeared with dirt and grime, and others may have used and abused you, but God's masterpiece remains untouched. No matter what you have gone through in your life, no matter what is happening now, God's love can weave a golden bond of restoration and redemption within you. Jesus holds out His nail-scarred hands and beckons you. In Matthew 11:28, Jesus said "Come to me, all you who are weary and burdened, and I will give you rest."

Someday, we will all see the God-created masterpiece beneath.

Acknowledgements

To my Savior, Jesus Christ, thank You for Your amazing grace. Thank You that You are the healer of the broken.

To my Heavenly Father, all glory and praise and honor to You.

To my sweet husband, thank you for loving me through the good, bad, and ugly of life. Thank you for being a safe place to heal and a fun place to enjoy life. You are a God-given blessing. I love you forever.

To Barbara Scott, thank you for your encouragement, wisdom, and editing genius. I am very grateful the Lord allowed our paths to cross. You are an answer to so many prayers.

Thank you, Jerri Kelley for pushing me to go deeper in the story. Stephanie Goble thank you for your help with the law office information. Jack Foster thank you for helping tweak the cover. Cathy Brewer, Lynn Mosher, and Cyn Rogalski, thank you for looking at some of the earlier drafts of the manuscript. I'm very grateful for your friendship, feedback, and encouragement.

To my precious friends and readers thank you!

About the Author

Lisa Buffaloe is a happily married mom, multi-published author, and speaker. When Lisa's not writing, she enjoys gardening, taking walks with her husband, and exploring God's beautiful nature.

Visit Lisa @ https://lisabuffaloe.com

Other Books by Lisa

Fiction
The Masterpiece Beneath
Nadia's Hope (Hope and Grace Series, Book 1)
  Prodigal Nights (Hope and Grace Series, Book 2)
  Writing Her Heart (Hope and Grace Series, Book 3)
  The Discovery Chapter (Hope and Grace Series, Book 4)
  Open Lens (Hope and Grace Series, Book 5)
The Fortune
Grace for the Char-Baked

Non-Fiction
Float by Faith
Heart and Soul Medication
Time with The Timeless One
The Forgotten Resting Place, First Place Finalist in the Bible Study category, Global Media Summit 2020 Christian Literary awards.
Present in His Presence
We Were Meant for Paradise
One Lit Step: Devotions for your journey
The Unnamed Devotional

Flying on His Wings: Living above daily struggles, taking flight with God
Unfailing Treasures
No Wound Too Deep for The Deep Love of Christ
Living Joyfully Free Devotional, (Volume 1) Finding Freedom, Hope, and Joy in the Journey
Living Joyfully Free Devotional (Volume 2), The Joyful journey continues

I write *"not for professional theologians but for plain persons whose hearts stir them up to seek after God Himself."*—A. W. Tozer

Thank you for reading
The Masterpiece Beneath

Lisa Buffaloe